Born in the diverse country of Malaysia, Sanuja Nair spent the best part of her studying years in a cozy little country called Brunei. Drawn to reading at a very young age, she believes in the power and freedom that it gives to the imagination. Turning the pages of a good book is one of the best ways she spends her time. She currently lives in the vibrant United Arab Emirates with her husband, and she has two lovely daughters.

From my heart to the hearts of the Naughty Nairs, my Mum, my family and friends.

Sanuja Nair

DAWN TO DUSK

AUSTIN MACAULEY PUBLISHERS™

LONDON • CAMBRIDGE • NEW YORK • SHARJAH

ISBN – 9789948750239 – (Paperback)
ISBN – 9789948750246 – (E-Book)

Application Number: MC-10-01-1156099
Age Classification:17+

The age group that matches the content of the books has been classified according to the age classification system issued by the UAE Media Council.

First Published 2024
AUSTIN MACAULEY PUBLISHERS FZE
Sharjah Publishing City
P.O Box [519201]
Sharjah, UAE
www.austinmacauley.ae
+971 655 95 202

A big thank you to all my family and friends for the love and support and to everyone at Austin Macauley Publishers for their hard work and patience.

I left…in a fit of rage…*no*…not in a fit of rage…no…but a moment of depression, a moment of frustration, a moment of clarity….and now, I have gained something but at the same time, I have lost everything.

Growing up, I lived in a world that I did not want to live in. Happiness seemed to always be in the form of somewhere else with everyone else. What was wrong with our house? I could never understand it. Why we could not be happy like everyone else and why the fun in our house could never last for more than half an hour, was beyond me. It was truly frustrating.

For most of my life as a child, I cried myself to sleep out of sheer frustration at not being able to do anything about the position that I was in. I don't know what it was that I was hoping for but as kids you rarely analyse what frustrates you. You just know that something does and you just want to get out of it. You almost always wished you had some magical powers or something that makes you different from the rest of the world but nothing ever does.

So here I am, looking down at the air that separates me from life and death. One step and I can end all misery with the hope of coming back to a new life. Maybe the life that I always dreamed of having. I'm not even sure if such a thing is possible but the hope that it could be is definitely better than what I have right now.

Why have I not taken the step? Well…at this moment, three of my most favorite things in this world are stopping me.

The great sun that is setting at the very moment sending explosions of orange and yellow with a hint of deep red colours throughout the sky. No matter how many times I see it, I cannot help but feel the same way I feel every time I do. A sense of calmness runs through me. A strange energy seems to run through my body. I feel warmth and stillness. This is one of my favorite times of the day. I wish this feeling could last forever…

The wind, my absolute favorite, that is blowing around me makes the moment even more magical. Though it cannot be seen, it can always be felt. The sounds it carries with it from far away, the thoughts and whispered secrets of people moving with it and the smell of nature it brings along with it. A magical moment that sadly always goes as fast as it comes……

The water below me. The sleek way it moves past me. The changing colors of the water mimicking what's above through the day has always fascinated me. Right now, the reflection of the magnificent colours in the sky are moving along with it. In a little while, it is going to turn grey and then dark and as it is a clear day, there will be those little gold droplets dancing in it as they dance in the sky.

That is why I have not taken the step. Maybe my choice of time to leave was not as appropriate as I thought it would be. I should have chosen a time that means nothing to me. I wanted this to be special for me…magical…enchanting even, but the very same things that are making it these for me are the very same things that are stopping it for me. I am torn now. I want to but I'm afraid I will miss all this if I do not somehow return here.

Time is running out. The great sun is disappearing right before my eyes. Dusk is settling in. I love this time, this moment but I cannot take the step. Another thing that will not mean anything if this moment goes. My legs are not moving. My mind is thinking it but my body is just not reacting…

A small creak on the wooden bridge that I'm standing on gets my attention. My eyes are shut but I heard it. My heart is beating fast. I don't want someone else to do this for me. But who can it be? No one comes here. I know this for sure…No one comes here because I have come here for the past one month to escape a life which I wish was not a reality. Not a soul. I have always wondered about that. Why no one came to such a beautiful place? Why? It seems so ridiculous.

There's the sound again and it's closer now. I am going to take the step. No one is going to ruin this for me. I am trying to make my body react to the desires of my mind but it is being so stubborn. I start to open my eyes a little. I try to calm my breathing. I'm trying to block everything out of my mind. I'm trying to ease my body. I feel light now. It feels like some weight has been lifted from me from up above. I can feel my feet move. I suddenly feel calm. I'm going…happily…

"*Wait*…Please don't…"

My legs freeze again…no… no… no… please, feet…please don't do this to me. Please. I try to ignore the voice.

"Hey…please don't. Don't do it…"

God…who is this person? No one ever comes here and of all the days in the damn calendar, this is the day he chooses to come. Life really can't suck more for me now. Talk about Murphy's Law.

"Hey…look. Please don't do this. It's never a way out. Nothing good ever come out of this."

Great…not only has someone decided to come today of all bloody days…it has to be someone with a major in psychology. Just my freaking luck.

Hmmm…what should I do now? Just take the step to which Mr. Psychologist here, I'm sure will turn into a lifeguard and spoil my moment which is already spoilt or should I just turn around.

And just in the blink of a moment…like all my life, I don't have a choice again.

"Look…just don't do this okay. I just want to talk to you. Will you please move back a little? I'm not really that good of a swimmer but if you jump…I'll have to jump in too."

Great…add Mr. Titanic to his resume too.

I can hear him breathing. He is closer to me than I thought. I can smell him. My friend the wind is carrying his smell and twirling it around me. It's a very hypnotizing smell. It's really nice. Musky and perfect for the evening. But not this evening. Any other evening would have been nice but *no*…it had to be this evening…

The wind blows the scent again and gently swoops it under my nose. It's a very calming smell. I close my eyes again and feel the calmness. I smile. Then I shake my head as I cannot believe this day has not been over for me.

"How do you know what is it that I am going to do?"

"I saw your foot half way across the edge of the bridge. I just took a guess coz you sure aren't dress like you were gonna go for a swim."

"What do you want?"

"I'm not even sure. Talk maybe. Or even if not, I can't let you jump. As I said, I'm not that good of a swimmer."

"So, you've mentioned."

"Please can you move away from there?"

"Would you like me to go forward?" I'm smiling to myself picturing the expression on his face. I can hear him chuckling.

"Very funny. So, I'm just gonna come beside you and stand okay. I promise I won't do anything. I'm just gonna stand beside you."

"Yeah, well…I didn't think you were gonna push me in. And you can stop talking to me like I'm some psychiatric patient coz I'm not."

"I'm sorry. I didn't mean to sound like that. I just didn't want to…well…you know…make any sudden moves to shock you into falling over."

"That would have been a bummer for me."

Strangely, I could sense him smile. It's funny how you can do so many things you didn't know or were not aware of when situations permit.

"I'm going to sit at the edge of the bridge so don't pounce on me thinking I'm going to jump. Okay."

"Sure…would it be okay if I came and sat next to you?" he asked.

The smell of him was really getting to me. It was sending some unwanted shivers through my body. Strangely, it seemed to be a familiar smell and it was just hypnotizing.

"Only if you promise not to push me in." I laughed a little just thinking of his expression again.

"Yeah…okay…you have a deal."

The smile again.

So, there I sat and I could feel him get closer. I don't know what he looks like and well, he doesn't know what I look like too. I could feel him sitting next to me. I am staring down at the water, which is now as dark as the night and I can see little gold dots dancing in them. As it moves along, the little waves that move with it look like silver threads blanketing the water. It was such a pretty sight. My friend the sun had gone to wake another part of the world but my friend the wind remained to tease me with this stranger's smell. I can almost feel him smiling as he does that.

"It's a really beautiful night," he says.

"One I would not have seen had it not been for you so I guess I should thank you."

"I'm really not sure if you mean that or if you were just being sarcastic but I am glad that I made you see tonight."

We sat there quietly, just listening to the sounds of the world. The water, the insects, the owls and all that live in the night when we go to sleep. Only then do you realize what you miss through the night when you go to sleep. Beautiful things exist in this world both day and night. What a shame that we cannot enjoy them all.

A doubt flickered in my mind. Oh no…no….no…no…if not today, it will be tomorrow. This guy is not saying anything and yet, he is making me doubt myself. I am definitely not going to let that happen. But he knows this place. My perfect place. I'll just have to find another one. But I really wanted it to be perfect. I didn't want to make do but if I didn't have a choice, then I just might have to make do.

I am still staring down at the water and I can feel or I think he is staring out ahead at the trees.

I can hear him sigh which means the time has come for him to ask me the question that is playing in his mind. I know it is making him nervous. I know that he is trying to think of the best way to ask it without inciting anger in me. But the question will eventually come out. So, I make it easy on him.

"Ask."

He turns toward me and sighs.

"Okay. Why?"

"The only reason there ever is…to get out."

I'm waiting for the line of questions that will follow. The big talk on how there are other options and everything else that normally comes with a situation like this.

"Can I make a deal with you?"

Okay…that I definitely did not see coming. A deal? What deal could possibly be made for a few hours coz there will be no tomorrow for me.

"What deal would you like to make?"

"You talk to me for 16 days and if I haven't convinced you to take my hand, I will support you the next time to want to take that step."

I'm still staring at the water but just realized that I had stopped breathing for a while. I slowly bring up my head and turn toward him and look at him for the first time. He is still staring straight out and smiling. He is really gorgeous and that hypnotic smell suits him perfectly.

He turns toward me and I am just looking at him now. "Just talk?"

"Yes…just talk…so do we have a deal?"

"You are just trying to buy time that will not matter once it's up."

"It's okay. Whatever the outcome is, I am willing to accept it. Do we have a deal?"

I'm not sure what to say right now. My mind is racing. Why should I do this? I don't have to say yes but I seem to want to. *No*…I have to be strong and stick to my plan. I have to do what I set out to do. Handsome, nice smelling guys should not be allowed to change my mind. It is just not right.

He is still looking at me waiting for an answer and I am still staring at him not wanting to give one.

"Do we?"

I parted my mouth knowing very well what was on my mind. A big *N*…*O*…and I…I was just going to flat out say it. I'm sorry but no matter how handsome and nice smelling, things were not going to change for me. There was no purpose for this deal. It will lead to the same path anyway so what was the point…

Shaking my head, I smiled and said, "Okay…"

What the hell? My brain and my mouth don't seem to be coordinating at all…it was supposed to be *no*, not *okay*…oh my god…I can't believe I said that…

"Great," he said. "I'll be looking forward to tomorrow."

I am still in a daze as to how I said okay. Must have been that haunting smell of his. Wind…you are not my friend right now…

"So just talk, huh?"

"Yup…"

"No tricks?"

"None whatsoever…just plain, old fashion talk."

"Yeah…funny guy," I muttered under my breath.

"So, we meet at dawn?"

Dawn…my other favorite time of the day. I just never seemed to like the in between.

"Dawn it is."

"If I leave now, you promise not to jump?" he asked with half a smile.

Still gorgeous….

"A deal is a deal…I guess."

I watched him walk away from me on the wooden bridge till I could no longer see him.

Strangely, I seemed to be looking forward to tomorrow. I wasn't sure what I was going to tell him but I wanted tomorrow to hurry.

Day 1

I am there before the light of dawn. Sitting at the same spot I was left at the day before. Looking into nothingness. Just black. I can feel the cool wind. I love the feel of it. I can hear the trees dancing to the movement of the wind. I can't see them yet but I can hear them. It's amazing how your other senses come to life when one is deprived. I close my eyes, waiting…

The wind is giving me shivers through my body. It is not from the cold but from the excitement that I feel. I shouldn't be feeling this. It will not help me at the end of it. I'm trying to brush it aside and calm myself.

I take a deep breath…and that's when I knew he had come. The hypnotizing scent rises through my nose and sends waves through me. I open my eyes and straight ahead I see the first light of dawn, a deep orange against the fading grey of the night. At the very same moment, I felt him sitting next to me watching the first light of dawn.

"You're here," I'm trying to conceal my smile. I don't want to look too eager. I want to try to be as cool as I can but my annoying heart is beating and it feels like the whole world can hear it. I am wondering if he could too. I dare not turn to look at him just yet. I'm afraid that he can hear it. I am afraid that he can sense my excitement. It will do me no good.

"As promised," he says and lets out a soft calming breath.

We sit quietly for a few more minutes and watch the rest of the grey night fade into the background to give way for the blue sky and the white clouds. The wind still blowing to tease me with the hypnotizing smell, no doubt, but I can see the trees dancing now. I can hear the branches swaying into one another and I can see the sun reflecting its light off the leaves to make them look like they are shining stars.

What would morning be without the sounds of the birds. The chirpings and some even singing and those who are soaring the skies to their freedom…freedom…the very reason I was here yesterday.

"Why the sudden change of mood?" he asked.

"I'm sorry…what?"

"The sudden change of mood…why?"

I slowly turn to him. Stunningly gorgeous. I just want to pinch his cheeks, actually I would like to do a little…well…a lot more than pinch his cheeks but…not really the best of situation at the moment. But it scared me to think that he realized that there was a change in my mood after thinking of freedom.

"That obvious?" I ask.

"Hmm…nope…not that obvious. Only when you pay close enough attention and know what to look for," he said.

"And what is it that you are looking for in me?"

"Time will tell," he half smiled again. Just too gorgeous.

"Fifteen days to be precise," I half smiled.

"Then I'd better get started. Clock is ticking for me."

I'm waiting as I am not sure how this works. I'm waiting for a question that I can answer. I am not sure though what we would do the rest of the day after I have answered the question. But in all honesty, even just sitting here next to him seemed to be satisfying. I shouldn't be feeling all this but I can't seem to help it. It's just coming.

"When I was a little kid, I had this fantasy that one day while walking in the woods near my house, I'd find a mystical creature somewhere in it. I used to go in every day, every chance I could but always came out with nothing, other than the birds, insects and the occasional creepy crawlers."

"Really," I say. "Not one unicorn, a centaur or a fire breathing dragon in all those days. That's just a bummer."

He laughs and looks at me. "Don't be so cruel. I was a little kid. Okay…I admit…the fantasy might have carried on to a slightly more than kid age but…hey…a guy can dream."

"Yes…that you can…dreams are good…till none of them come true."

"Maybe some have but not in the way that you wanted or expected them to be," he turns away.

Oh my god. I have upset him with my negativity. God…why do I always do this. Why do I always see the more bad part in everything then the good in it? He was just sharing his childhood memory and I had to ruin it. Sometimes I can really be so stupidly stupid.

"I'm sorry," I say.

"For what?" He genuinely looks surprised.

"For being a little negative."

"Everyone is entitled to be negative sometime or the other. I just think that you should not let it consume you. So, don't worry about it. But tell me, what was your fantasy as a little girl?"

I start to give out a loud chuckle…

"I'm not sure that you are ready to embrace the journey of my childhood fantasy, Mister."

"Bring it on, young lady," he winked.

I realized at that moment, as soon as I said it, that I actually did not know his name. *Should I ask now? Hmmm…never mind, I'll leave it first and get to it slowly…but surely…*

"Ok…my childhood fantasy…let's see…"

I stare ahead at the dancing trees and the sound of everything around me. Then I close my eyes and I can feel him look at me…I can feel his stare…it takes me back to a moment in my life…which is possibly the best moment of my life and I smile to myself just remembering it. Remembering it like it was yesterday…the exact same feeling running through my body right now as it did that first moment…

But that's not the story for today…

"I used to wish that I was special. I wished that I had some powers in me that would one day make me special. I hated being the ordinary nobody all the time," I said.

"So, when I was small, I used to fantasize about being a fairy queen. And don't you dare laugh about it." I turn to him and squint my eyes. But he is not laughing.

"I'm not…"

"But you wanted to," I challenge.

"No. That would be hypocritical coming from someone who is still hoping to find a mystical creature, wouldn't it?" he said with his both eyebrows arched.

"True that…"

"So, tell me, what type of powers did you wish you had as a fairy queen?"

"I always imagined that one day, I would suddenly discover that I had the power to talk to nature. As queen, I imagined that I lived high up in a tree castle decorated with many different types of flowers whose different scents filled the castle with calmness and peace. I would have all my little fairies living around me in their own homes along the branches of the tree. We would look after nature."

"That is really interesting," he said.

"I had a drawing of my tree castle when I was little. Always kept it with me."

"Where is it now?"

"It got thrown away by someone who didn't understand what that drawing meant to me."

"I'm sorry," he said.

"Yeah, well…sometimes people just don't understand the value of your childhood even if it's just imaginary. Some imaginary stuff really takes you through your difficult times when the world seems like it's gonna crash in on you."

"Yes…I know…believe me."

"So why flowers?" he asked.

"I don't know. I just love them. I love the colors of the different flowers. The smells they give. They are so pretty. They seem to light up anything they come into contact with. For example, you know when you look at grass…it's just plain green. Don't get me wrong, I love the greenery too. In fact, green is my all-time favorite color. But when you add little yellow flowers growing through the grass and you see them swaying with the wind, suddenly the grass has a different life altogether…I really don't know how to explain it. Let's just say that I am one of those who'd rather spend money on flowers then gifts. They just really…really make me feel happy."

"Wow… now I'll never look at flowers as so ordinary and as just flowers again," he said playfully.

"Real funny."

"You know, there were times when I was little when I would feel sad or frustrated, I would wish that I could close my eyes and fly into the night to another dimension. I always imagined that dimension to be acres and acres of land filled with green, green, grass with little yellow flowers dancing on them in the wind. And trees after trees with all sorts of different colored flowers," I sighed. "Sadly, nothing like that ever happened. I remained in my home living every moment of sadness and frustration that used to grip me. I really hated that feeling."

'I'm sorry your childhood was not what you wanted it to be'

I smile more to myself.

We got to talking about so many anythings and everythings and at times just nothings that I didn't realize that dawn had turned to dusk.

I knew he had to go but I really didn't want him to go but I couldn't stop him. I didn't want to look desperate. Besides, I was married and have two kids. What I am feeling is just not right.

"Same time, same place tomorrow?" he asked.

"Yup…" I nod and smile though I felt a tinge of disappointment.

With that, he slowly gets up and walks away.

I close my eyes wanting to look back but afraid that he'll see me looking. Oh well…what the hell, I turn…and…he is nowhere to be found.

Day 2

As fast as he disappeared at dusk the day before, he reappeared at dawn.

I find myself smiling at the smell of his perfume. Some form of familiarity was creeping in but I can't quite place it. It makes my heart beat faster. It gives me a tingly feeling. I take a deep breath and open my eyes.

Just as promised, he is there at my side at the break of dawn.

I looked at the sky to see the first break of light. Today, it seemed like someone had taken a paint brush and painted the sky with different shades of blue. I don't think I ever knew that there could be so many shades of blue. In between all the shades were fine waves of orange with a touch of yellow. It's amazing what nature does on a daily basis.

Many of us wake up and do not even spare a minute to the beauty around us. We are so busy moving…moving…moving with our lives that we just let nature pass us every second of the day…till now, I cannot figure why that is. I am guilty of it as well. But now…with all this time…I seem to see…what happened to time for me? How did it not become a constrain for me anymore?

Because I made it not…that's why…

"So deep in thought?" I heard him say.

I smiled. "I'm just wondering where did my time constrain go. Why do I have so much of time in my hand?"

I turn to him in time to see his jaw tighten. Just for a split second. Or maybe I just imagined it.

"We can never just enjoy what we have. We always seem to want to question things that are given or taken. I guess that's part of the human nature. Unable to gain satisfaction at any time," he smiled.

"I guess you are right. Even when we are satisfied with one thing, something else will always find its way to come up and make you dissatisfied again…just a vicious cycle."

He turned towards me. I could feel him staring. I want to turn to meet his eyes but my head just won't move. *C'mon*…I'm telling myself. *Turn…just turn*…but I can't. I close my eyes and realize that I'm not even breathing. Slowly, I let out my breath and start to breathe again. Then I open my eyes again.

I finally turn my head but he was not looking at me anymore. He was staring straight ahead like he did most of yesterday. How strange. I just couldn't understand why I didn't turn. I wanted to so much but just couldn't.

"So," he said to break the silence. "Tell me what you enjoyed doing with your family when you were younger."

"Ummm…" I sighed. "Let's see. There weren't many things we would do as a family per say but…"

"What do you mean?" he asked.

"Well, we would go to friends' houses when invited, birthday parties, parks and outdoor activities and such but it was always when we were invited by someone or it was organized as a group thing. We never really did do anything that was specific to our family."

"Oh…I see…"

"Anyway, the one thing that I liked that we did do as a family was go on drives to see the twinkling colored lights that people had put on their houses for festivities. Even when the streets were lit up, I somehow felt really happy to see them. I don't know why."

"Twinkling colored lights huh?" he seemed confused.

"Hahaha…it's stupid but…"

"No…it's not stupid. I'm sorry that you thought I had thought that but no…I didn't. It's not stupid. I was just wondering what twinkling colored lights you were talking about."

"Ahhhh… You know, the lights like those ones people would put up on their Christmas trees, the twinkly ones. Many would decorate their houses with those lights during festivities and I just loved watching those houses. They all looked so cozy and nice. Sometimes I just wished that I was in one of them."

He caught the sadness in my voice. I could feel him looking again. I didn't want to cry so I continued, "Some houses would have one themed colour and some would have multiple colors. It was just strange to me that I felt different emotions when I saw the different colours. I really don't know how to explain them. It's like, different colors of the twinkly lights, affected different emotions in me. I always thought it was weird. I always wondered if anyone else felt the same way but dared not ask. I was scared of being made to look silly."

I turned to him in time to see him smiling.

"Why are you smiling?" I asked him.

He just shook his head.

"What is that supposed to mean? You think it's silly too?"

"On the contrary, my dear,"

A wave of shiver passed through me hearing him call me that. Oh God, I hope he didn't sense it. *What the hell is wrong with me? I have a husband back home and I am getting excited at being called "Dear" by another man. How much more shameless can I get. What in the world is happening?*

But I try to play it cool.

"Meaning?" I asked.

"I will explain in due time" he said.

And I'm thinking in my head, *Are you kidding me? Really?*

And as though he sensed what I was thinking, he said, "Really, I will…now tell me more."

"Nothing more to tell. I would always wish that it was our house but it never was," I sighed.

"Why?" he asked realizing that I had sighed really loudly.

I shook my head. So many things were playing in them. So many frustrations that just wanted to come out but nothing did. It all stayed in my head. Anger was building inside of me. I just wanted to scream. I just really wanted to scream…*why? Why could it not be? Why could it not be our house?* Would never have gotten an answer anyway.

We must have sat in silence for a very long time because it felt like dusk had come in the blink of an eye. I felt like I literally just closed my eyes for a few seconds and I was watching the sun lazily go down the horizon and I knew what that meant.

He must have sensed my disappointment.

"I'm sorry. I ruined the day," I said with my head down.

"You can make it up tomorrow," he said in an almost whisper.

I felt even more bad that he had agreed that I had ruined the day. I was hoping that he would say, *no you didn't* or *it's okay.*

I shook my head, slowly trying to fight back tears. I closed my eyes again and heard a whisper in my ear, "No…you didn't."

I could feel his breath and smell his scent near my ear. My neck tickled and again a shiver was sent down my spine. My heart was racing and my hands were trembling but when I opened my eyes he was gone.

I looked back to see if I could catch him walking away but he was just gone. Just then the wind blew and I caught his scent. It woke the butterflies in my stomach. The trees were swooshing in the wind making sounds with the leaves. I felt a nice cold whiff. I felt that it was okay. I didn't ruin the day after all.

And now, I have to go to where I don't want to be…

Day 3

Don't cry...Don't cry...I told myself. So, what if they don't want to speak to you. So, what if they are angry with you for leaving. Just so what.

I can understand him. But not my babies. Why would they be so mad to a point of not answering me? But I don't blame them. Maybe I should have thought about this before storming out of the house.

The pain I must have caused them. But I just could not bear it anymore. I just couldn't live a life of lies. I couldn't pretend to feel the things that I didn't feel or not feel the things that I could feel. I just wish someone understood.

"Why the tears?" he asked.

God, I didn't even realize that he came. I didn't realize that I was tearing. *How am I supposed to explain this now? Uggghhhh...hate it when people see me cry. Really hate it...*

"You have got to stop doing that or I am going to get a heart attack and die of sheer shock one of these days," I smile.

"Ha...ha...ha...don't want that to happen for sure," he said, but had this weird look on his face. Not so much weird look as it was a side smile. "What are you sad about?"

I wasn't sure that I was ready to share that much of privacy with him yet though he really made me feel so comfortable. I feel that I can just blabber anything to him but I shouldn't. I should keep somethings back for when or if I do get comfortable enough to share it with him.

"Okay. No problem. You don't need to say anything. You can tell me when you feel comfortable to do so. Let's talk about something that would make you happy."

I am beginning to wonder if he is some kind of mind reader. He always seem to know what I'm thinking. Or maybe it's just my expression that gives off what's on my mind. Or… maybe it's just perfectly logical that not everyone wants to share private things in their lives with someone they have only met for four days.

I smiled. He turned to me. "So, what makes a pretty girl happy during her childhood?"

"You really know how to flatter a lady," I said but couldn't help grinning. It was nice to be called pretty girl. Made me feel ten years younger.

"Well, let's see…I guess I could say school."

He was looking at me with one eye brow arched, "Really…"

"Ahhhh…but don't get me wrong. It was not the studying bit for sure that made me happy. Well…okay…not really true to say that. I did enjoy some of the lessons when we had the good teachers. But mostly it was all the other stuff that we used to do."

"And who is we?" he asked.

"We is…my best friend and me."

The world's greatest best friend. That is the best friend I had. Sometimes I wished there was a time machine that could take me back to 'those days' minus a few parts of it. She was the one that made everything else bearable.

Without having to say anything to each other, we somehow always knew exactly what one was thinking.

We had planned this big getaway from school once and it turned out to be the best day of our lives. Till today, I don't know how we pulled it off and till today I don't know what I would have done or where I would be if I had been caught. Facing the school disciplinary would have been a walk in the park compared to what would have happened at home. Believe it or not, it still sends shivers through my spine just to think of it and yet at the same time, it brings the biggest smile on my face when I think that we did it.

It took one month of planning. Thankfully, Sheyna stayed close to my home. My parents liked her a lot so we were in each other's home quite often. Me in hers most of the time. It was my escape route. Excuse was always, we needed to study. We did study though, just not all the hours that I was there.

On the day of our great escape, we tried to be as normal as we could. My heart was pounding the whole time in the house and I was so scared that my dad or my mum would hear it. I tried to do everything I could as normal as I could and not hurry time. I wanted to leave the house the same time so I don't look too excited to leave. I was never really a morning person and the prospect of leaving the house for school wasn't really appealing every day. Thank god for Sheyna. It made it a little easier.

At exactly 7:00 am, I said my normal goodbyes to everyone at home and headed for the door. We walked to school or rather we walked toward school but never got to school. Unlike schools today, if you were absent then, there would be no phone calls to your home to find out why you did not come to school etc. Mobile phones weren't even invented then so it kinda made life for these things a little easier. All you needed was a letter from your parents the next day to say why you did not attend school. Somehow, we got that bit sorted out as well.

First thing we did was to get to the public toilet near the school and get out of our school uniform. We then changed into our casual jeans and t-shirt and got sun hats to make it look like we were young tourist. A little makeup always helped to jack up the age and we were set to go.

We hopped on the public bus and paid for our fares to the next town. It's not that the place we lived in had nothing exciting to do but we had to do this adventure somewhere where no one would recognize us.

The bus ride was initially worrying for me. Sheyna wouldn't have gotten into as much trouble as I would have and she knew it. There were many times when she tried to talk me out of it knowing what would happen if the plan did not succeed but I was very insistent. I told her that for once, I just wanted to be free. To do something that I will remember for the rest of my life. Something that I could tell my kids that I did instead of always having nothing.

She understood. She let me be worried for as long as I wanted to be. Our journey would take around half an hour. We didn't want to go too far so we could enjoy the day. It did help that we said we had a study group and would be back around 6:00 pm. So, we almost had the whole day.

I was quiet the first ten minutes thinking of all the excuses I could give if caught. Then I looked out of the window and thought to myself, *Hell, I'll think of excuses later.* I am going to enjoy this one day. That's all it took to sway my mind. Sheyna and I spent the next twenty minutes talking about anything and everything. We didn't make too much noise as most teenagers would. We didn't want to attract any attention to ourselves. We didn't want to talk to anyone or we didn't want anyone to talk to us. We just wanted it to be us.

Since we were by the coast, the ride was really pretty. The sea and lots of greenery. I loved every minute of it.

We reached the next town on schedule. Our first stop was a café to have breakfast. A nice café. We both came from average backgrounds. Not too rich but not too poor either. But it was one of those situations where most always got better things than us. So, money was not easy to come by. We had made a pact to safe half our allowances for four months and we would think of what to use it for when the time came and that time was now. Strangely, we both got the same amount of allowance so we saved the same thing. And we stretched out to the fifth month when this plan came about. We had a decent amount for the day if we worked it out well.

The main bus stop of the next town was very close to the beach which was our target. In fact, it was just beside the beach. There were many small cafes along it that had this homely touch and feeling to it. We started walking and found a nice cozy one to have breakfast in.

The lady behind the counter was the typical grandmother running a café image that you would have. She was really sweet and pleasant. Turned out, she owned the place and all the pastries and cakes were made in her kitchen under her watchful supervision. "I ain't having none of them factory rubbish here in my store," she said with a smile but full of conviction. We knew that we had chosen the right place for breakfast.

Sheyna and I both agreed that we would have a big breakfast to last us for most of the day and that's exactly what we did. It was a really nice feeling to just be free for the day. We talked and ate and talked and ate and talked some more. The sound of the waves was like soothing music. Strangely, I felt like I picked up a pattern of sound from the waves. I don't know if Sheyna did as well. I never asked her.

The weather was perfect. I just felt that on that day God was just on our side.

We had our breakfast and the kind old granny even threw in a cake for each of us to have as dessert. "When you're on holiday, what the hell," she said and we burst out laughing. What the hell indeed.

We thanked her and started to walk out toward the beach. We, of course, did not have any books in our bags. We had our towels. And our school uniform which we changed out of. Our swimsuits were under our current outfit so we were good to go.

As we were walking, a gush of cool breeze moved past us and I really had a strange feeling. I suddenly got a shiver run down my spine and my whole body tingled for a few seconds. I stopped and looked around but I wasn't sure for what.

"Hey," Sheyna said. "You okay?"

"I just…I just…"

"You just what?" she asked. "OMG please don't tell me you saw someone we know or someone recognized you coz we'd be so dead."

"No…that's not it…I just had this really strange feeling that's all. I really can't explain. C'mon let's go…time is ticking…don't want to waste it."

We set our towels out. These would be donated or thrown out, of course, as no traces of sand can ever make it to our houses or it would be a disaster. More in my house than hers though.

I was never really a fan of the afternoon. The ideal time of this adventure for me would have been from dusk till dawn. That would have been perfect but when you are not in a position to choose you just go with the flow.

We talked most of the time about our life. What we were going or at least what we would like to do once we were out of school. I believed that Sheyna would have done the things that she wanted to do as she had the full support of her family but me, I knew what I wanted to do and then there was what I was expected to do. That was the frustrating part of my life.

We swam, talked more girlie talk and dried ourselves in the sun which was not too hot. It seemed liked we picked the right day. Coincidence? Maybe, or God was just on our side.

I think we might have slept off a little while coz we both sounded like we lazily woke up. Sheyna looked at her watch and said that it might be time for lunch. We were still kinda full from the huge breakfast and the free cake so we decided on ice cream. Why not, right? We were supposed to be enjoying the day after all.

We packed our things up from the beach and walked toward the cafes. I vaguely remembered seeing an ice cream parlor while we were looking for our breakfast venue. As we were walking, we actually saw a sign saying, *If you would like to donate your used towels, kindly put them in the space below. It would really help someone get through.* There was a yellow bin below the sign. Sheyna and I looked at each other. "Perfect," we said together and started laughing.

We saw many tourists relaxing and enjoying themselves. The great thing about being on holiday is that you never have to worry about time. It is never a constrain. It's just a shame that it never lasts. Somehow you just have to get back to a time constrained life. So annoying.

"There," Sheyna pointed.

"Yup, that's the one I saw," I said.

We walked toward the ice cream parlor and again, I got that strange feeling. Shivers down my spine and I suddenly had butterflies in my stomach.

What is going on with me?

This time I didn't say anything to Sheyna. I didn't want to freak her out.

We walked in and lucky for us, it was not too crowded. Most people were out still enjoying the sun. But we had to time ourselves so we could get back in time. We were keeping close eye on the time.

Sheyna was choosing the flavor that she wanted and was making small talk with the lady behind the counter.

The butterflies in my stomach got stronger and something drew my attention and I turned to face the door and that's when my heart just almost stopped. Someone was watching me. I didn't realize I was holding my breath until he gave me the warmest smile I've ever seen from a guy. I really cannot remember if I smiled back or not. I just stared at him and before I could react, Sheyna called me.

"What happened? You look like you've seen a ghost."

"The guy outside the door," I started to say but stopped when I turned my head and he was no longer there. No, I could not have imagined it. I know I saw him.

"Never mind," I said.

We bought our ice creams and sat on the patio of the store. I kept trying to look around to see if I could find him but he was nowhere to be seen.

We finished our ice creams and because it was a forbidden day, the ice cream somehow tasted better than any other day.

"Hey, I need to use the rest room for a bit. I saw one back there," she pointed.

"Okay. I'll wait for you here,"

The best day of my life and it's coming to an end. The clock is ticking and the sun is slowly heading toward the horizon of the sea to usher in one of my favorite time of the day. Dusk.

"A penny for your thought," a voice said.

I must have really looked like I'd seen a ghost. "I…uh…I um…," I couldn't even get words to come out of my mouth.

The butterflies were back and I was trembling. I was just staring at him. He was the most handsome guy I've ever seen. He was just so right. Everything about him was right. He smiled and I fell off my chair.

"Sorry, I didn't mean to make you uncomfortable," he said.

I took and deep breath and let it out and got myself together.

"Please, don't apologize. You are certainly not making me uncomfortable. I just got a bit of a shock when you suddenly appeared in front of me. I was sort of looking around for you after I saw you there," I pointed at the door of the ice cream parlor.

"Sort of looking for me? Were you hoping to see me or not to see me?" he smiled.

I smiled back and closed my eyes. I looked at him and said, "To see…I don't know why but your smile seemed to have captured my attention."

"Honest and straight forward. I like that. It's a good characteristic to have."

"Thank you," I lowered my head and stared at my hands that were on my lap.

"Not from around here I presume," he said looking out to the sea.

I just really wanted to kiss him then and there but it would have been a little too straight forward.

"Ummm. No."

"It's a really nice day to be out though," he said.

"Yes…it almost seems perfect." And it was to me. God, he is so handsome I can't even bring myself to look at him.

"I have to go now. I'm on duty. I'll see you around," he said.

'Oh okay…but how will you know where to find me? I don't even know your name. You don't even know mine, "I must have sound really disappointed. I was. Not disappointed but devastated. I really wanted to plead and beg him to stay but with some ounce of pride I did not."

He smiled. Damn that smile. It just melts the heart.

He stood up. And I smiled. "It was really nice to meet you though it was very brief. You really have the most charming smile," I told him. I just had to.

"Thank you. It was nice to meet you too."

He walked to me and sat beside me. My heart was beating so loud that I swear he could hear it. His shoulder just slightly touched me and I was seeing stars. I really thought I was going to faint. I closed my eyes and I heard him.

"I will find you, life after life, if I have to," he whispered in my ear.

I let out a deep breath and opened my eyes. I was not tearing but my eyes were wet. I turned around to see him walk away but he was nowhere to be seen again. He just disappeared.

Day 4

"So, did he come looking for you as he promised?" he asked.

I think he could sense my extreme disappointment. I just stared down at the water. Still dark turning light grey and then shades of orange and yellow as the first light bursts its way through the sky. A nauseated feeling comes. Just at the moment, I felt like a loser. I was back in high school again.

It was too early in the morning for tears. Just too damn early but I could not stop it. I tried really hard but they just kept coming.

"Hey, I am really sorry. I didn't mean to…" he started to say.

I had things in my head that I wanted to say to him but nothing was coming out of my mouth. It's like my eyes have taken over my whole head. Nothing was stopping the tears from falling down. I felt so embarrassed.

He handed me his handkerchief. I took it. It had his smell all over it. Somehow it made me smile. I felt a little calm. I blew out a deep breath and thought to myself that if I am going to get this out of my chest, it might as well be to a stranger. At least when Day sixteen comes, I would have told everything and hopefully, I can go with a light heart.

I looked up at the sky. The pain in my heart and the knot in my stomach made this part of my life story difficult.

For the first time, I looked at him and I really looked at him. I don't know his name. I don't know where he is from. I don't know who he is and yet, here I am comfortable as hell to tell him stories that I have not shared with anyone else in my life.

Maybe that is what makes this easier. The fact that I do not know anything about him and neither does he know anything of me. Maybe that's why I should tell him all of it. After Day sixteen, I really do not care what he does with the story. I will not be around to find out anyway.

The knots in my stomach turned into butterflies when he turned to look back at me. I wanted to say something but I was choking up.

"I'm sorry," he said softly. "I'm so so sorry to have made you cry."

"There is nothing for you to be sorry about. It was a question anyone would have asked given the story that I told."

For just a split second, I thought I saw a sudden sadness pass through his face. It was a curious thing. Maybe he knows what I felt. Maybe he had gone through something similar and could empathize with what I had gone through. Then it would be so much easier to tell coz he would understand. He would understand and know exactly how I felt. I wouldn't seem so crazy after all.

"The answer to your question is sadly *no*," I finally said. "I never saw him again, ever and I really don't know why it affected me so badly but it did. This total stranger. Someone I had never laid my eyes on. Someone I didn't know.

Someone whom I have no connection with whatsoever. But it affected me so badly that he never tried to see me again."

From the corner of my eye, I could see him look to the sky but couldn't understand what was it that made him look a little sad. The girl that might have done something similar to him. That must be what.

"What are you thinking of?" I asked.

"Nothing," and as soon as he said it, he knew coz I let out a laugh. He laughed a little too.

"I was just thinking that it must have been hard on you to have waited."

"Hard? No…painful? Yes," I said.

Growing up where you have no say over anything takes a toll on you. Never being allowed to think for yourself. Never being allowed to make decisions that affect you and the life that you want to lead, never being allowed to choose what you really want for yourself really hinders your ability to do the things that you want to do.

It causes a lot of insecurity within yourself. . So you grow up your whole life thinking that everything has to be decided for you. You are too scared to make any decisions and you are terribly afraid that the decision you make will be the wrong one.

But little do you realize that these are the very reasons that eventually end up making you make the mistakes that you try to avoid.

My self-esteem as a child was always low. I just grew up thinking that I was just not enough of anything. It was really annoying actually.

So, when it came to the matters of the heart, I guess I was just lost.

"I'm sorry," he said.

"What for? You didn't do anything. It's not like you were the one who left me," I smiled.

There was something in his smile that I just couldn't put my finger on .

"I shouldn't be bringing bad memories up for you."

"But that's the whole point of this, isn't it? You wanted to know why I was so ready to jump of this edge. Well, this is part of it. Bad or good, it is a part of it," I said.

"Yeah…but I am also supposed to be trying to convince you *not* to…not encouraging you to do." He looked at me and smiled.

"Well, intentionally or unintentionally you have halted that process for sixteen days so I guess you can somewhat call it a little convincing not to."

"True…" he nodded.

Day 5

I closed my eyes knowing exactly what would happen at the break of dawn. The break of light and the familiar smell. I know it's stupid. I've only known him for four days but there's just something so familiar with him. Actually, I'm not sure if there is or if I just want there to be. I seem to be forgetting that I am still married but something just feels right. And again, I am not sure if it does feel right or just me wanting it to feel right.

He could be many things. He could even be a serial killer for all I knew. Maybe just trying to gain my trust so it will be easier. A panic chill rose up my spine. I hadn't considered that at all. I just sat there with him for the past four days and talked about my life. I should be more careful. Should I just leave? Should I stay? Omg…what should I do?

Something was not right. I had all these things running on my mind and didn't notice that the break of dawn had passed. It was getting brighter now. I could see the sunlight through my closed eyes. But, where was he? I didn't get the familiar smell.

I slowly opened my eyes hoping with all my heart that he would be sitting there. I couldn't feel anything next to me. I didn't want to turn my head and face the disappointment so I just looked sideways and there was no one.

I don't know why I felt so rejected. I don't even know why it hurt so badly. I just closed my eyes and shook my head. I didn't feel like going home. I put my head on the floor and wondered if I should sleep or if I should jump.

"You cannot possibly do this. I cannot do this," he said.

"You have to," said the deep voice.

"Why? Why do I have to? What good can come of this? It is only going to push her over the edge faster. She might even try to do it today," he sighed.

"She must want to not do it herself. If after all your talk finishes on her day sixteen and she chooses to still go ahead, then she cannot be saved anymore," said the deep voice.

"However, if she does not take that step today, then there is a greater chance you'll be able to save her. I have never failed in guiding you though at times it might not be the way you see fit. So, I am asking you to trust me."

"You know I do. You know I trust you with all my heart, Master," he bowed his head.

"But I am scared. I am scared to be the one who let her down yet again. I know she doesn't know it but I do and it will kill me within to know that I have done it again."

"Trust your mind. There are other ways to communicate with her. You do not have to physically be there to make her understand."

He could sense a smile in the deep voice. His Master. His guardian. Though he has never seen him, he knew deep within his heart that his Master was right. And he has never failed him in any way. And that's just how it worked.

He glided out of his Master's abode and set out to seek a quiet place. There were plenty of quiet places when in need. At times when he thought that none was available, some place would suddenly free up. Just like today. So, he closed his eyes and began to focus on her.

I finally saw him walk towards me. My heart was racing and I knew that I was smiling. All my disappointment had just melted away. He had his head down and he was taking slow steps with both hands in his pocket. As he approached me, he looked up slowly and smiled. I wanted to run and give him a big hug but I thought that would be a little too much.

"I'm sorry I could not make it today," he said.

"Oh, no worries. You are here now so we're good."

He smiled. We sat in silence for quite a while. Just taking in the wind and the sound of the trees dancing in the wind. Catching the sunlight bouncing of the leaves making it look like the trees were glittering. It was really beautiful.

It took me back to my reality. These were the things that I enjoyed doing at times but I could never understand why my husband was always so impatient to leave. We would be at the beach and dusk would be slowly enveloping the area. Cool breeze would whiz by and I'd close my eyes to enjoy it, only to have him ask me to hurry up and pack our stuff.

Sometimes, I would ask him why…and he would just look at me like I was crazy. I often wondered how it was that we were so similar but so different in our ways. There were a few characteristics that we had in common but we were so different in our interests. At times it was really frustrating.

"Hey, can I ask something of you today?" he broke the silence.

I was taken aback but "Sure," I said.

"I want you to promise me that you won't jump today," he said.

I could see that he really meant it as he was staring straight into my eyes and I swear I felt the pierce. In a good way though.

"I…well…yeah…okay…sure," I said rather stunned. Not so much for the request but more so for wondering how did he even know that I had thought of it.

I looked at him and he must have seen my curiosity.

"Hey…how did you… I mean why would you suddenly…"

And at that moment I felt a gush of wind sweep across my face and opened my eyes. Dusk had come. I looked around and found myself lying on the floor of the bridge.

I slowly got up and looked around again. There was no one. I had been asleep. It was a dream. He didn't come. *OMG…but it felt so real. It felt so so real.*

I fell asleep the whole day. Could I have? I must have.

I suddenly felt a chill when I remembered the promise I made. *Does it count. I mean, it was a dream. Does a promise in a dream count?* Just at that moment, a second gush of wind surged through me and my mind told me that it counts.

I closed my eyes and whispered to myself, "I'll see you tomorrow."

He smiled. His work was done. He bought another day. His Master was right. Now he felt there was more hope.

Day 6

Punctual as always at the break of dawn. I'm still amazed at how he is able to do that every day at the correct moment. Like magic.

But I am more worried of how the anticipation of the break of dawn is making me feel. The shivers it sends down my back. The butterflies fluttering in my stomach. And all those tingly feelings you get when you just begin dating the boy that you've been wanting for so long…

OMG…this is not right. Not right at all. I have a husband and two kids at home. What am I doing? How can I feel this way? But I don't seem to have any control over it. It just comes even when I try not to think about it.

I'm so scared to open my eyes now. I know he is there beside me. I can smell him. And that is making me tingle even more. My eyes are starting to water out of excitement. *OMG…what in the world am I doing here?* I start smiling in my head. *No, stop that. I'm not supposed to be smiling in my head or at all.*

"Are you planning to open your eyes at any time?" he asked with a smile I could sense.

And I don't know why but I burst out laughing. And so did he. It was really nice. I felt so free. It felt like my laugh came from the heart. So genuine. For a few seconds it felt so great to be alive. Whoever would have known that a simple laugh can have such a great effect on anyone. It really felt so good.

When I finally stopped, I realized that he was simply smiling and just looking at me.

"I'm sorry. I really don't know what overcame me. I wasn't laughing at you."

"I know," he said. "It was just really nice to see you laughing so much. You looked really happy. Genuinely happy."

"Strangely, I really felt that. Genuinely happy. Whatever that means…but for a fraction of a second, I just felt free."

He smiled to himself.

"Really crazy huh…to think that such a simple thing could affect you in such a way," I said while looking up to the sky.

"So…which part of my life would you like to discuss today, Mr. Nosy?" I smiled.

"Hahaha…that's really funny…I've never been called Mr. Nosy before but if it serves its purpose…then Mr. Nosy it is…well…hmmm…let me think. What indeed shall we talk about?"

I could see him make the thinking face with full frown on his forehead and squinting his eyes at the same time. I shouldn't be feeling what I'm feeling now. It's just not right. Not given the situation that I am in.

I know that the longer I sit and talk to him, it's only going to get more and more out of control. *What if something that shouldn't happen…happens? What will I do then? How will I explain? How will I walk away from everything? But at the same time…how can I go back to anything now?*

"Let's talk about some happy memories you and your best friend have had."

"Happy? Hahaha…Sheyna and I only have naughty memories. but yeah okay…those naughty memories made us very happy."

He smiled.

Damn this guy…he is definitely not making things easy for me.

"You can start whenever you are comfortable," he said smiling.

I didn't realize I was just staring at him. At his face until he said that.

"Yeah…well…let's see…what can I tell you about Sheyna's and my adventure that is safe," I ask more to myself and smile.

We had a lot of happy times. Most of my happy times were spent with her. I always felt like I could just be myself.

We'd spend hours talking about anything and everything. And I mean literally everything. It's amazing that you can be at that much ease with someone as I was with Sheyna.

I guess now when I think about it, I really have got to be so thankful that she was there. I mean, we were never in competition about anything. I didn't care if she was better at some things than I was and neither did she if I was better at something than she was. We would always help each other out. Believe it or not we have never, ever fought a day in our lives.

"That's really strange isn't it?" I sighed.

"Well considering that you two are girls, that's really something. I've known sisters who fought for absolutely nothing and end up not speaking for years. Such a shame really."

"Yeah…we weren't like that at all. We couldn't stand not talking to each other. We had too many things to update on. And you know, there weren't handphones or internet or any other form of communication so we needed to talk to each other. I mean there were the landlines but you really didn't want everyone listening in on your conversation so we met all the time and talked all the time."

I don't think I actually told him an incident that made me happy coz with Sheyna, I was just happy. It's really difficult to explain. There aren't many best friends who go through life being best friends till present but she and I, we are still that.

"So…what happened?" he asked.

"What do you mean?"

"What happened to her? Where is she?"

"Nothing happened to her. She's around and we still talk."

I think I knew where he was going with these questions but I really didn't know how to answer him. I haven't spoken to her since I left the house and one day is too long for us. She doesn't even know where I am.

A pang of guilt circled my stomach. I suddenly felt like the worst friend ever. *How could I have done this to her?* I was about to do something so horrible without even talking to her. My God…I was going to ruin everyone's life.

"Hey," he called.

He must have sensed that I had realized where he was going with the questions. I kept my head down.

"It's okay…we all make mistakes."

"I didn't even make an attempt to call her before…," my voice trailed off.

"She's gonna be so disappointed in me."

"Don't beat yourself up. Sometimes things might not be what it seems."

What did he mean by that? But my mind was too distracted to ask. I just kept thinking of how I did not even attempt to call her. She must be quite upset. Worst of all, *How would I call her now. What would I say? Where do I start?*

Day 7

I smiled at the break of dawn…the smell…his smell…oh God. this is just not right. I should stop this right now before things get worse…but what things? Will it get worse or could it maybe be getting better…*oh my god…what am I thinking…*

"A penny for your thought," he said.

"You'll be really rich. I have so many things going on up there just this instance. You might just be able to quit whatever job you have and lead a good life."

He laughed. So, did I. Not sure why though. I really didn't think it was that funny.

Then we fell silent but not an awkward silent. It was a pleasing silence. The rustling of the leaves in the wind bouncing the morning's sunlight off made it look like they were covered in gold glitter. It was so pretty to see. And the wind…just the right amount of wind…I have always loved the wind. So much comes to live even with just a little bit of wind. I often wondered if anyone thought the same. If anyone really appreciated the wind? You hear people appreciating the sun, the moon, the stars…but I truly wonder if anyone appreciates this creation of nature that cannot be seen but can make you feel wonders.

What am I going to miss in a few days' time? I am going to miss so much. I am going to miss everything. So why do I keep wanting to do this? Why have I not changed my mind? Why has he not given me the urge of changing my mind? I seem to want to be with him the next few days but I also want the days to pass so I can finally do what I came here to do. But why? Why do I still want to? My mind is racing…I close my eyes and calm my mind…the answer is simple…the answer is in the question…would everything miss you?

"Are you okay?"

My thoughts broke. I knew I was gonna tear up. I choked, took a deep breath and turned to him, smiled and said, "Yeah."

He nodded.

"I did go by her house you know," I said, maybe coz I didn't want him to think that I was that bad of a friend.

"And?"

"I walked up to the front door. I stood there for a while and just asked myself…what would I tell her? What would I say to her? How am I going to tell her that this is what I've decided to do and I'm sorry but no matter what you say, I *am* going to do it."

He looked down into the water. I am not sure but it seemed like his expression had changed. It looked like he was disappointed. I am not sure if it was because I did not have the courage to go through with seeing my best friend and owning up to what I wanted to do or if it was because I was going to do what I set out to do. I felt bad looking at him. A little bit of guilt as well but I don't know why it was still not enough for me to tell him…you know what, I've changed my mind…coz I hadn't…at all.

"I'm sorry," I sighed.

He looked at me curiously. I must have read his demeanor wrong. I must have got it all wrong. Stupid me.

"Why?" he asked. Naturally.

"Umm…I just thought…well…I kinda thought that maybe you were a little disappointed that I did not go through with seeing my best friend…*oh my god*…what the hell…why did I even admit that. I'm stupider than I gave myself credit for…I really just wanted to knock my head somewhere."

"Hmmm…no…not disappointed that you didn't see her. I understand. It's not easy. I mean, what would you actually tell her? Maybe you need a little more time to think about it to decide what you would say to her."

"Yeah," I said feeling a little confused.

"You know, we've been through so many things together and she reads me like an open book. She has never second guessed me. Always very supportive no matter what stupid things I wanted to do or the things that I should have done but did not want to do. You know what I mean?"

"Yup…we all have those moments."

"But…this one…this one is the one stupid thing I need the most support and I know I will never ever get it." I shook my head and looked at the running water.

The shadow of the leaves in the water and the little twinkling on the surface of the water caused by the sun rays were just so beautiful. Just made you want to jump in and flow with it.

"Well can you blame her?"

"Huh?" I looked at him.

"Can you blame her for not wanting to support what you intend to do. I mean, turn the situation around and ask yourself…if she was the one who came to you looking for your blessings to take her own life, would you give it to her?"

Well when he put it that way, it sounds positively stupid. What am I expecting of her? Who in the freaking right frame of mind would give their blessings to someone who is relatively healthy to take her—own bloody life. God…I am just being so so stupid with this but why can't I tell myself…*no…*

"You are absolutely right. No matter how much I might understand her reason for doing so, I would never ever tell her to go ahead and take that step. It's the people who are left behind that get hurt the most. Coz you…you just go… but everyone else is left behind to understand and seek answers they will never find."

He smiled. It wasn't really a 'yeah…now you might change your mind' smile or a 'finally…I think I got through smile' but more of a 'glad you understand but…' I can't quite make out what the 'but' is for. It just felt a little strange.

Maybe I'll attempt to go again. *But what would I say to her. How can I explain this and make it right?* It only seems right to me but no one else would understand.

We fell silent again. Just sitting there and watching the sun cast it rays and watching the leaves bounce them from tree to tree with the help of the wind. I felt like I was sitting in a gold dome of sun rays. It felt so warm with the wind brushing over my skin like an invisible silk blanket. I love the wind.

But time seem to pass so fast in this place. I don't know what it is but sometimes it feels like it takes ages for the sun to go down and sometimes it just feels like it's gone in the blink of an eye. Another strange thing. I can't quite put my finger on it.

And just like that, the day was finished. I seemed to have lost track of it. I really don't know how many days I've been coming here and just sitting down with a stranger and telling him things I probably shouldn't while my family is back home managing themselves.

I should stop this. I should be home. I should be doing things for them and yet I don't feel the urgency to go home. I don't feel the need to go home. What is happening to me?

"You'll figure it out soon enough" he said breaking my thoughts.

"How'd you know what I was thinking?"

"Doesn't take a genius to figure it out," he smiled. "You've been wondering about everyone around you and it's only natural that you would be also wondering what to do or what to say to them."

"I guess you're right. I hope I figure it out very soon."

Coz it's really killing me inside. I just want to burst out screaming and I just want to cry my heart out but I just don't know what's stopping me. I just want to be free from these feelings.

I watched him walk away waving to me like he always does and disappearing at the very same spot he always does.

I turned around and closed my eyes. My friend the wind was back. I took a deep breath and I had this inkling feeling that I would not be seeing him tomorrow.

Day 8

I am not sure what made me go to Sheyna's house today instead of my usual place. I just had this feeling in me that he would not turn up today and I guess I just didn't want to be disappointed when he didn't. I was not 100% sure that he wouldn't turn up but was very close to it. But the biggest question in my head was…why do I even care?

A strange feeling swept through me. I was scared but at the same time excited. I mean, I am after all married with two lovely kids but I don't know why I feel like it's time I took the step.

Oh my god…what am I thinking? Eight days ago, I was ready…really ready to take that step down but now here I am thinking of taking a different step… No…no…no… this cannot be happening. Am I? Am I really? Am I really starting to change my mind? Oh no…this can't be happening. Has he really done it? Has he changed my mind?

I shoved the thought past me. I refused to think about it. And now I am planning to go to Sheyna's house. What if she talks me out of it? What would I do then? I can't go back home. Not after the way I left.

And *he* never said that he was trying to talk me out of it to be with me. *Oh my god…I have assumed too much. It's me. The feeling is mine. Maybe I won't go back there tomorrow or ever. I should just leave right now…right this moment when I can…*

But my legs kept taking me to Sheyna's house. My mind wanted to do something else but my legs kept walking there. Before I knew it, I was standing at the gate of her house facing her porch. I always loved her porch. It looked out to a beautiful garden. She was always so good with her garden. It was just so full of flowers and I loved flowers so much. The sight and smell of them, all different colors and many different scents just brings a certain warmth to my heart. It just feels like heaven.

I could see her sitting on the porch staring out to open space. The sun was throwing its rays in all directions but strangely it was not hot. The wind as always was blowing a light breeze. Maybe that's why it was not so hot. I could hear the trees rustling from the wind and could see the flowers dancing a slow sway almost as if they were putting up a show for us.

It was such a lovely day. So beautiful. One that Sheyna and I would have gladly taken advantage of when everyone was out for the morning. We would have sat on that porch. Had our coffees and talked and talked while taking in the scene of the trees and flowers and feeling the warmth of the breeze as it gets thru the sun…

But not today…today on this glorious day…I am here to bring her the worst possible news. To tell her what I am going to do in a few days' time. What kind of a friend am I? What am I doing? Can anyone be this cruel?

Would anyone understand why? Could your bestest friend in the whole wide world who has shared everything with you from childhood possibly understand why? And I started thinking to myself...would I understand why...would I actually understand why...

What if I was the one that needed to understand. How will I look someone in the eye and say...you know what...I do understand...you do what you gotta do. How and why would you even say that to someone.

Oh God...this is just wrong. This is just not right at all. I wanted to take a step back but I couldn't but at the same time I couldn't take a step forward as well. I was just stuck there. Stuck to the ground. What was happening? Why couldn't I move?

Then you remember what everyone keeps telling you to do in situations like these. Do they ever work? No one really knows but can't help to give it a shot. Nothing to lose anyway.

So...I close my eyes, take a deep breath and count to ten. As the number three...two...come to my mind, the cool wind blows soft across my face and I open my eyes at once...

At the same time that I take a step, a stronger wind blows and the trees sway faster and the leaves rustle louder. The dried leaves on the ground strangely made a cracking sound like when someone steps on them and I look down and realize that I had taken a step forward.

I look up and see Sheyna staring straight at my direction. I'm not sure what to do now. She looks really mad. She looks pissed as hell. My heart is beating so fast I'm almost choking on it. Then I realize that I've held my breath when I saw her staring at me. I slowly start to breathe again and come whatever may, I have to do this. I owe it to her.

I had barely taken three steps and I heard her scream.

"Stooooppppppppp…just stttoooooopppppp…"

My heart literally stopped.

"How dare you? Just how dare you?" and she could not finish her sentence before gasping for breath. She had run down from the porch and was almost a few feet away from me. Just staring at me with so much of anger.

In all my years of knowing her, I have seen her get mighty pissed at some occasions but not ever like this one and I cannot blame her one tiny bit.

I'm still frozen. I want to move but I can't seem to take the next step. Count…damnit…count to ten and take the step. It's going through my head but my feet are just not bloody moving…

"How could you?" she finally says. "After all we have been through…how could you?"

I am just standing there staring at her literally like the cat has gotten my tongue. I want to say something but my mouth is so dry and I can't seem to open them.

"For god sake…*I am your best friend…your best friend,*" she screams in so much of pain. *"your best friend,"* she says again crying softly in so much of pain.

I watched her go to the ground, crying the way she was, in so much of pain, I just finally realized what I had done.

Tears were streaming down my face and I was chocking in them at the same time.

She looked straight at me as I sat down at the same spot where I was standing. I wanted to run and give her the biggest hug but I didn't think that she deserved me as a friend, let alone a best friend.

Just seeing her hug and cry herself rocking back and forth with that much pain…pain that I had caused, I just couldn't take another step to her knowing that there was nothing that I was gonna say to make it any better.

What can I tell her to make it better? What can I say? I still haven't changed my mind so what could I explain? How can I change my mind? Where would I go? My husband and kids will never accept me after I stormed out the way I did. How can I live anywhere knowing that they are somewhere hating me? I just could not cope that with situation, even worse knowing that I brought it all upon myself.

I cannot fix this…

My heart is in so much of pain now. It's like a gripping pain. I'm choking with tears. I feel like I cannot breathe…and there's no one there to safe me. Suddenly I feel scared…my heart starts beating fast. I feel like I am having an anxiety attack. I can almost hear my heartbeat…

And these words keep playing in my head… there's no one to save me…there's no one to save me…

Just at that moment, Sheyna looks at me…she's sobbing… "Why did you not tell me? Just why? I would have helped you…I would have done something…I would have done anything for you…all you had to do was ask or just tell."

The guilt that I felt made me just want to run straight to the bridge and jump off…and at that moment also, it crossed my mind that if this is how she was feeling…what the hell am I putting my husband and two kids through. They don't deserve this. None of them deserve any of this.

Shamefully, I plucked up the courage to look at her, searching my brain for something to say but nothing was coming. I could see her looking at me just waiting for me to say anything.

"Please," she said. "Please just say anything so I can understand."

And there I was, just sitting there and staring at her like a full-blown dummy. Coz really…what do I say…what can I say…

And yet again, I find myself closing my eyes with tears just streaming down, the stabbing pain in my heart…and counting to ten.

I open my mouth to say something…

"Just don't…" I hear her say. "I don't even think I want to know and frankly I don't even think you can explain."

With that, she just stood up, looked at me on the ground and looked at the sky and shook her head and walked away.

As she took her first step, I managed to open my mouth, "Please…don't go…just let me…"

And I knew she wasn't listening as she walked off. She put both her hands up and gave a dismissal wave, like people do when they don't want to hear any crap explanations, shook her head and again looked to the sky and walked off…forever…

"Explain," the word that I ate while she walked away.

And just like that I blew my chance with my best friend as I have with my husband and kids and again I feel alone…and the reality of it hit me so bad…I am alone now…I have turned away from the only people that I have had.

And at that moment…I knew exactly what I was going to do as I walked to the bridge. I have a little time left before dusk…

"I cannot let her do this. Please master, please let me go to her," he pleaded.

"Do you trust yourself?" the deep voice asked. "Do you trust your feelings 100%?"

"I don't know. I just don't want to lose her again. I have been waiting for lives just to be with her. If I don't go to her now, it will all end."

"Do you think she will take the step?" his master asked. "What does your feeling tell you?"

"I can't concentrate on my feeling. I just can't concentrate at all. I'm watching her go in utter disappointed. A feeling that can push anyone over the edge."

"Have I not taught you anything?" the deep voice asked calmly.

"You have taught me everything. I know there's much more for me to learn but right now I don't know if I have enough to take me through this."

"Always trust your feelings. I have taught you to communicate. Maybe it's time for you to put it into practice. Bring yourself to calm down first. Let there be only one thought. Free yourself of everything else and communicate."

Only a few more minutes to reach. If I cannot face her, if she is this upset and angry with me, how can I face my family. My husband and two kiddos. They will never understand. I know that once I am gone, they will still never understand but at least they will move on with their lives after some time. At least that is what I am hoping for.

There are many, in fact I think probably everyone, who will think of me as being selfish but they don't know what I am going through. They don't know what it feels to be trapped. No one will understand what it is like for me.

Almost there…

Promise or not…*Oh god…promise…that's what I did…I promised. Why did I promise? Why did I promise a total stranger?*

Why should I care about this promise when I am breaking every promise that I have made to anyone and everyone? Why should I care? I'm not even keeping my promise to my husband and kids. So why in the world should I care about this stranger?

Because you know the end game and you owe him that much. He doesn't know the end game but you do.

I am already there…I am at the edge. It's just one step away. Just one step to go. I close my eyes and I take a deep breath. I can feel the cool wind swirling around me and just as I am about to take that step, a familiar smell plays around my nose…

"Oh no…how can this be possible? How can you come right at this time? How can you possibly know?"

I shook my head and looked at the water streaming past calmly below me…I smile to myself knowing that he will not be there but yet I just cannot take the step…because I promised.

I sigh deeply…the familiar smell becomes a little stronger and I still know that he will not be there. I just sit at the edge of the bridge and look up to the sky thinking to myself… what is it with you? What is it with you that makes me care so much about a promise that might not even mean anything.

"Always…always…trust your feelings. They more often than not never let you down," said the calming deep voice.

"Thank you Master. I am still learning."

"She will wait for you but from now you need to do what you have to do. Time is running out. You will have to tell her soon," he said.

"I understand, Master. I will."

I knew he will come tomorrow. Something in my heart made me feel that he will come tomorrow. Maybe that was part of the reason why I did not move. Maybe that is why I could not do it. I did not want to disappoint him. I did not want him to think that I was just a cheat. Someone who made a promise and never intended to keep it. But why should I care. That is what I just could not understand.

Day 9

It's only been a day but funnily, it feels like I haven't seen him in ages. I'm not sure what it is. Maybe it was the exhaustion I felt after leaving Sheyna's house or maybe it was both that and the awful pain that I have in my heart and the pit of my stomach leaving there with all the things that she said and most of all seeing the hurt that I have caused her.

I cannot imagine, what it must have done to my family. No wonder they don't speak to me anymore, no one would even look at me anymore. My husband, my kids…it's like I do not exist to them.

Was my leaving the house so bad? None of them knew where I was going. None of them knew what I had intended to do. *So why are they all so angry with me? Why are they so mad that they will not even speak to me anymore?*

I leave the house when it is still dark and no one even cares. My husband doesn't even ask me where I'm going or where have I been when I get back. *Does he somehow know?* I can't think of how he would though.

Maybe that is why I'm still standing at the edge. Maybe that is precisely the reason why I haven't taken the step. Maybe that is the reason why I care so much about the promise…Because he cares. He cares that I do not jump off. He cares that I stay for sixteen days. He cares.

I slowly sit down at the edge of the bridge with my legs over. The water is too low so my feet cannot touch it. I watch the water flow. It is still dark but in the flowing mass of black below me, I can see a faintish orange reflection slowly appearing and I close my eyes and just waited as the wind blew the familiar smell around me.

I knew as soon as I opened my eyes that he would be sitting next to me. I was just about to when suddenly a shiver ran down my spine and a thought crossed my mind.

I braved myself and slowly opened my eyes and sure enough, he was sitting next to me. I smiled and looked into the flowing water. This time it was clear as crystal with shiny gold drops bouncing along with it as the sun awakes the world for yet another day.

"I'm sorry," he said.

"For what?"

"About yesterday. I'm sorry I did not come," he smiled.

"Don't worry about it. Strangely I kinda had a feeling that you would not come so I did not come here either."

"Oh," he said sounding surprised. "What did you do then?"

I took a deep breath and slowly let it out. I didn't know if I wanted to tell him coz I felt so shitty about it but I needed to tell someone. I guess I was looking for some sort of validation for what I was thinking of doing.

"I…uh…" I shook my head and looked back at the water. I was already starting to tear up just thinking about it. I feel so embarrassed. *How do I tell him?*

"Don't want to talk about it?"

"It's not that…I really do but thinking about it is making me tear up and I know what is going to happen when I start talking about it."

"You know," he said. "Sometimes you might start off tearing but as you go along you might find yourself getting stronger."

"That's true, I guess."

"But if you are not comfortable talking about it, you don't have to. We can always talk about something else and you can tell me this story when you feel comfortable to do so."

I smiled.

"I went to see Sheyna yesterday. It didn't go as planned. Okay…not to say it didn't go as planned coz I really did not have any plan when I went there. But let's just say that it did not go well…at all."

"Oh dear," he gave a slight sympathetic smile.

"I probably deserved it," I said. "I mean, what kind of a best friend takes a decision without talking to the most trusted person in her life first. But you know, what would I have told her? What would I have said? I really don't think there's any way anyone could have discussed this with anyone."

"Can I just give my two cents worth here? I could be wrong," I could feel him look at me.

I smiled. "Go ahead."

"I agree with you. I don't think anyone ever discusses this and that is why the family members are left stunned and shocked when they find out. But I think, and this is just my thought, she's probably sad and upset that you did not tell her what you were going through to take such a drastic decision. And she's probably also upset with herself that she did not see something wrong. She's probably beating herself up thinking what kind of a best friend she was that she could not see what you were going through."

"Hmmm…you are probably right. I didn't think of it that way. That's probably how I would feel if it was the other way around."

Nothing was said for a while. We both seemed to be lost in space just looking at nowhere and thinking of nothing. The sound of the water just flowing past us.

This place is so perfect. For the everyday that I have come here, there never seems to be a day that has gone that wasn't like the perfect setting. It almost seems unreal. It's like one of those made up places in your mind. You know, you tell yourself you wish you were in such and such a place, wishing you could see the morning as how it was in your mind and the rest of the day to pass by just how you want it. It's quite strange actually. I wonder if he feels the same way.

Time seems to play around here as well. Sometimes it feels like we sit there for hours talking before the sun sets and sometimes it just feels like we've been sitting for less than that before the sun sets. Today is one of those days.

It didn't feel like my story with Sheyna was very long but then again, it might have been. My husband used to always say that I can make a one-hour story from a ten-minute situation.

My heart aches. My stomach knots. We used to have so much fun talking about things. At least I used to. He would listen and then poke fun at me for not having a full stop in all my stories. We used to laugh a lot. Where had it all gone wrong? Where did it all take a drastic turn?

I knew, of course, but it's a scenario that I will never bring up with my husband. He would never understand when it came to this. He would never understand the amount that it had hurt me and even worse, the amount it had hurt me when he did nothing about it. He would just brush it off as he always does with anything that I feel or with what I go through.

"You alright?" he asked me.

"Yeah…just something that ran through my mind for a split second."

And then I thought of another thing.

"You know, when I went to see Sheyna and we were exchanging words…or rather she was venting out how she felt while I just froze like a cat had bitten off my tongue, there was a moment, when I was trying to talk to her, where she just looked through me. I mean, I was trying my best to put in a word or two to try and explain but it's like she did not hear me."

I looked at him. "I didn't realize how angry she was. I knew she would be but I didn't think it would be of this magnitude. It's like she completely dismissed me. It really, really hurt that time. I felt my heart hurting at that moment."

He looked at me with such sadness and sympathy, I just wanted to burst out crying but I held back.

"I'm not sure what to say to you. I can only imagine how you feel but then again, maybe I can't. Maybe you should just give her some time. I'm sure she will come around eventually and understand that maybe it wasn't by choice. Maybe she would finally see it the way that it is. Sometimes all we need is just time to accept certain situations and time will help us move on," he said with a sigh.

"I guess you are right. Perhaps I should just give it some time. I will go back to her and try to make things right before…well…you know…"

I looked straight into the flowing water and felt the breeze flowing through me. I don't know what it is about the wind but every time I feel it, it somehow gives me the notion that everything is going to be okay.

"Same time tomorrow?" he asked.

I looked up at the sky and saw the dusk dawning. I smiled and nodded my head.

"See you then." He gave the top of my head a little rub and my heart started beating frantically. I looked up at him and he smiled and gave me a wink and turned to walk. The butterflies in my stomach were flying uncontrollably and my eye started to water out of excitement.

Omg...what the hell just happened? Oh no...no...no...no... I can't feel like this. But it was so exciting to have these feelings again. But no... I can't...I shouldn't...oh God... what is happening?

I closed my eyes and smiled to myself. I felt like an excited teenager. I turned to look at him once more but he seemed to have just vanished. I couldn't have turned around for more than one minute and I am sure it definitely takes more than that to walk to the start of the bridge. I definitely did not feel him run. Maybe there was a shortcut somewhere. It's the only possible explanation.

A shiver ran down my spine as darkness closed in.

Day 10

Something was bothering me and I couldn't quite place my finger on it. It was more like bits and pieces of things that has happened in the past two to three days and one that seem to happen every day for the past ten days. It's vaguely there in my mind but maybe I am just scared to give it a second thought or think of it as a possibility. Afraid to go there. Afraid of where it might lead and afraid of the outcome of it.

Maybe if I don't think of it, I will not have to deal with it. After all, I have just another six days left and then I don't have to deal with anything.

I felt a hand on my shoulder.

"Hey," he said. "Deep in some thought?"

Dawn was breaking.

"Sneaking up on me as always," I smiled as I turned and looked at him.

There was just something about his smile that was so comforting and so familiar.

"I don't sneak up on you. You just never seem to notice every time I come coz you are always in some deep thought."

"Not true," I said.

He smiled. "Okay. I promise to make more noise when I come tomorrow to announce my arrival."

"Hahaha…okay…I'll be looking forward to it."

He sat next to me. "Are you not bored of this place yet?"

"Hmm…I never really thought about it or it never crossed my mind actually. Now that you have mentioned it, strange isn't it?"

"Maybe it's because you have something to look forward to and that's why it doesn't bore you."

I looked at him.

"Oh no…oh gosh…that's not what I meant…"

I just burst out laughing and I couldn't control myself.

"Oh my god…my stomach is hurting and my eyes are literally tearing up."

"Well I'm glad that you are having a ball at the expense of my awkwardness," he said curling his lip to one side.

I was still laughing but somehow seemed to notice that he looked very handsome while he curled his lip.

And he finally broke into a big smile and I just wondered to myself if maybe what he said was true. Maybe his smile was what I looked forward to everyday. Maybe the reason I wanted to come every day was to see him. God knows I really enjoyed being with him. I really enjoyed talking to him. I really enjoyed laughing with him. All of these simple things that I really enjoyed that somehow did not seem to exist in my world anymore. Maybe I've been longing this for a long time. Maybe I just wanted to be me again.

When I finally settled and stopped laughing, he placed his hand on mine. My stomach knotted immediately and I think for a split second, I stopped breathing.

"I'm sorry," he said and gave my hand a little squeeze before he let go.

I was a little disappointed. I know I shouldn't be but I couldn't help it.

"I'm sorry. I didn't mean to imply that you were looking forward to coming here every day for that reason. It's not what I meant at all."

A wave of relief crept over me. I almost broke out into an uncontrollable smile. Thank god I kept it in control. He wasn't sorry he held my hand. That's what I was happy about. I shouldn't be but I was.

"Oh," I said. "Don't worry about it. I knew you didn't mean it and I am sorry I laughed so much. Your face when you thought what you had implied was just too funny."

He smiled and shook his head.

"Anyway, you are right though. I guess because I have something to look forward to, this place doesn't bore me. And, I sometimes feel that it somehow has a different charm about it everyday, one of those strange but true scenarios."

"How do you mean?" he asked.

"Well, I'm sure it's not true coz it cannot possibly be true but I feel as though there's something different about it every day. Sometimes it's the way the dawn breaks in, sometimes it's the way the breeze feels, sometimes it's the way the trees sway with the breeze, sometimes it's the way the water flows, sometimes it's the way the rays of the sun shines, sometimes it's the way the gold lights bounce off the leaves when the sun shines and sometimes it's the way the dusk comes in. It seems different every day. Does that make sense?"

"I don't know. It's just difficult to explain. I mean, it's like when you go…say…to a particular restaurant every day, you know how the waiter is gonna greet you, you know what's on the menu, you know the ambience, you know the cost of the meal but here…it's different everyday."

"Like I said. It's weird and I just don't know how to explain it. Maybe it's just got to do with looking forward to something when I come here."

"Maybe it's both," he said.

And I nodded my head. Yeah… maybe it's both or maybe it's just you. It shouldn't be but it was. That was naturally said in my head.

We both fell quiet. The breeze commanding the trees to sway to its movement, rustling the leaves as it flowed through them. I love the sound of the rustling leaves but not as much as I love the feel of the breeze. Whether it is hot, warm or cold, it always transports me to a time in my mind that I can never place is real or just imagination.

"Why do you love the breeze so much?" he suddenly asked distracting me from my thoughts.

Puzzled, I looked at him. "How do you know that's that I was thinking?"

He looked at me from the corner of his eye and gave a small smile. Then he turned to me and said, "I didn't know what you were thinking coz I am not a mind reader but I am very observant and I have noticed that you react every time a gush of breeze passes through. It's like you savor the moment. Your eyes close and your face becomes serene with a soft smile. There's a certain calmness that come to you and I was just wondering why the breeze and not the sunlight or the sound of the water or something else."

I don't know why but I felt a little embarrassed at his observation and I could feel myself blush. My cheeks suddenly felt hot and my mind was absolutely blank. I wanted to answer him but no words were coming out of my mouth. And then I realized that I was smiling to myself like an idiot. What he must think of me now.

I took a deep breath and cleared my throat to make it look like I was taking some effort into thinking of my answer.

"I…uh…" I finally looked at him and asked softly, "Do I really do that?"

And he answered in the same soft tone, "Yes, you do."

That was enough to set my whole face on fire. I was just hoping that he would not see how much I was blushing and shivering out of excitement at the same time. *But*…this is just not right…it cannot happen…it should not happen. I want to stop myself but at the same time I don't want to stop myself.

This feeling in me. How he makes me feel just by his sheer smile, I want it back again. But I know that I will never have this. Is it wrong for me to want this? Is it wrong for me to want to feel alive again? Is it wrong for me to want to blush again and feel special?

I know relationships evolve after marriage but I have seen my friends who have been married the same many years as I have and I have seen their husbands with them. Many of them still have that little spark in their marriage from time to time. You see the little things that go on between them, sometimes it's the little jokes, sometimes it's the playful ways they disturb each other, sometimes it's just a small gesture of sitting next to one another's arms.

"Hey," I felt a light squeeze on my waist. He had his arm around my back and on my waist. "Are you okay?"

I wanted so much to lean in and put my head on his shoulder but I was so afraid to move. I was so afraid to move because I did not want him to take his hand from my waist. I just did not want this moment to end. *...what the hell am I doing?*

"Yeah, I'm good. Just enjoying the moment." And as soon as I said that I just wanted to smack myself on the face.

I didn't realize how close he was sitting to me. I was trying to think if he had been sitting this close to me all this time and I just did not notice, but no, there is no way he ever sat this close to me. His hand came off my waist but it remained behind me as he was leaning with both arms behind him.

*Oh noooooo...oh noooooo...oh noooooo....*dusk was coming and I really wished I had some magical powers to stop time. *Oh please. I don't know if this moment will come again and I really want it to...I really do.*

I knew he would leave soon. I don't know what made me pluck up the courage and ask him, "Will you come tomorrow?"

When he straightened himself, I felt a little of my shoulder leaning on his and I felt that soft squeeze on my waist again as he whispered, "Of course I will. I'll be here for the next six days."

With that, I felt the palm of his hand slowly brush against my back as he stood up, turn to me and gave a little wink and smile and walked away.

And I really wanted to watch him go. I wanted to see where he went so I could follow him but I didn't. I don't know why I did not. Actually, I think I do know why I did not. I was afraid. I was afraid that I what I was thought might be a reality and I did not want it to be.

So instead, I closed my eyes and felt the breeze again for what could have only been less than a minute and turned around....and just like that, he was gone.

"She's walking back to a life that she will never have again. She has nothing there."

"I know," the calm and soothing voice said. "But you must be patient. Patience is the key to everything."

"I am really trying my best. I look at her and I just want to spill everything out. Every day that I see her there, it's every day that I feel this guilt of knowing and not telling," he said to the voice he calls Master.

"She's afraid of knowing and this is why patience is everything. Everything when done at the moment that it is supposed to be done, will fall into place for you, for the both of you," the master said calmly.

"I understand, Master. I just hope that I have done enough to change her mind," he said.

"Time will tell. You need to go and prepare yourself well. The next few days are going to be critical. It is as how they would put it...make or break."

He knew his master was right. He had to make it right. He has to succeed. Not succeeding is not an option for him.

It would have been so much easier if she hadn't chosen this path, but she did so he had to prepare and he had to prepare well.

Day 11

I felt my shoulder resting against his and as always, I did not hear him come. I smiled and opened my eyes to a wave of pink and orange merging in the sky with the help of the breeze to form what looked like nature's best work of art.

"Beautiful isn't it?" I said as I let out a breath and relaxed my shoulder on his. I don't know what gave me the courage but the phrase 'seize the moment' popped into my head. Something which I have always never done. Everything was always calculated with too much of thinking. The moment was just never seized.

"Yes, it is very beautiful. Much like the lady sitting next to me."

I instantly turned to see him stare out in the sky and smile and then turn to me.

"I was always taught to give praise where it is due."

"Well, then thank you. You are too very handsome," I blushingly said.

He laughed as he touched my nose playfully and said, "Funny too."

"I can see why this is one of your two favorite time of the day."

"And what is the other?" I said really puzzled now.

"Dusk."

My heart started racing. It's too early in the morning for this. We just started the day. Please don't ruin it…please don't ruin it. One part of my mind was racing to somewhere and the other part was racing to pull me away from it.

"Ummm… why do you say that?" I asked.

"Simple, you come here Dawn and you leave after Dusk," he said. "If I was not here forcing you to stay during the middle part of it, my bet is that you would go away at midday and probably return at dusk. I could be wrong though."

Okay, my heartbeat started slowing down. *Yes… that is a very simple observation. He has been with me almost every day of the eleven days and it is only logical for him to know this.*

"Well, how do you know I don't stay here once you leave at dusk?" I smile as I ask.

"A good guess. Was I wrong?"

"No…not at all. You are right. As much as I really like this place, I don't think I have the guts to sit here on my own through the night although I might as well do," I said the last few words as softly as I could and hoped that he did not hear it.

And once again, we were just sitting there and staring into space though he did not seem as calm as he normally does. If anything, he seemed a little agitated. Just a hint of it. Or at least that's what I felt. I could have been wrong.

He took a deep breath and let it out. Then he turned to me and held my hand. The jolt that it sent up my body was unbelievable. All the butterflies in my stomach just knotted and I went very still. I was trying so hard to control my breathing and make it as normal as possible.

I really don't know what he was feeling. If he felt the same as me or if he was just taking advantage of the situation and I wasn't sure why I was so much at ease to not even question him. I certainly did not take my hand away. If anything, I just wanted to move in closer to him but I froze as always. I just froze.

"So, what went wrong?" he asked and I just looked at him and shook my head.

"What went so wrong that it brought you here? To the very end of this bridge? To want to take that one step into the water?"

After eleven days, he finally asked the question that I was dreading. Just another five days and I would have been done with it. Would I have been done with it? I'm not so sure now. But what choice do I have now. I cannot go back. No one even acknowledges me at home. It's like I don't exist. I was just waiting for these five days to finish before deciding on what to do.

My palm started to sweat. My breathing started to get a little heavy. My face suddenly felt hot and my heart started to beat like mad. I took my hand off his thigh and started wiping both my palm on my thigh. I really thought I was going to pass out.

He must have noticed how uncomfortable I was getting. He put his arm around my waist and gently told me to take a deep breath and close my eyes. And before I knew it, my head was resting on his chest and he had both arms wrapped around me. We stayed like that for a few moments and I slowly pulled away. I felt calmer now and I knew I couldn't avoid this question any longer. If not today, it will be tomorrow and if not, it will be the day after.

"It's a long story, but then again maybe it's not that long after all."

He looked around and jokingly said, "I don't have any place to be right now. Take your time and tell."

I chuckled more to myself.

"You have to understand that my husband…he is not a bad person at all."

"Hey…I'm not here to judge. I'm not even here to pass any comments. I'm just here to listen."

I nodded.

"Hmmm…" I sighed. "Where do I even start?"

"My childhood wasn't the best. It wasn't the worst but it definitely wasn't the best. I know that as an adult when we look back, we always think to ourselves…well, it could have been worse but as a kid that thought never crosses your mind. You always looked at the kids who had it better and think to yourself, well, if only you could have it that way too.

"In my house, your opinion as a kid was never wanted. You were told what to do and you did it without questions. At that time no one saw the impact this would have on a kid like me. See, I was not the rebellious one at home. I was more of the obeying one. I didn't like to be told off or shouted at so I always did what I was told.

"Sheyna's house was different. She was the only kid but I don't think that was a factor in anything. Her house was always full of conversations between her parents and her. They used to do things together all the time and always had fun doing them. She almost seemed to have had the perfect childhood. Well, at least in my eyes anyway. In that way, I used to envy her but it never came between our friendship.

"In a way, I think it shaped her up to be the kid that she was. Bubbly and full of life. The greatest advantage I had was that my parents liked her a lot and so using her name was my ticket to the little freedom that I had. Every chance I could, I would go and spend time at her home in the pretext of doing homework. But I had to be careful and strategically plan myself so as not to be seen as trying to get away from my house or it would have been the end of that for me.

"I always felt that nothing in my house lasted. Like, happiness was not allowed to last. If we were happy about something, in a split second everything would go downhill. I really hated those situations and never understood the reason for it.

"All my childhood growing up, all I ever wanted to do was run away. I just wanted to get away from a situation that I felt so trapped in. A situation that made you feel useless. That you were not good enough for anything. A situation where you could not fulfill your dream of becoming anything coz everything that you wanted was always met with a negative respond or just not allowed.

"My only consolation as a child was that I knew I would grow up someday and will be able to leave and live the life that I wanted to live. But unfortunately, I was not bold enough to do it.

"Having been brought up with that mindset, I always kinda ended up taking all the paths in my life to fulfill the happiness that was not mine. At some point I probably should have stopped that mindset but, I don't know… guess I just never did or never quite realised where my choices came from".

'Don't be too hard on yourself', Shaking my head softly, a tight knot in my stomach formed. "And this sadly spilt over to the person that I chose to get married to. Don't get me wrong. It wasn't an arranged or forced marriage but I sometimes wonder if deep down, I chose to get married to him because it was a way out for me. You know, thinking maybe now, I can start living my life. For this reason, until today, I hold that guilt of making this decision as I feel that it was a selfish decision for me to make at the cost of someone else's happiness or what could have been his happiness.

"He is a nice person. At the beginning, it looked like we had so much in common but as time went by, I started to realize that our interest were not very similar. If I wanted to do A, he would want to do B. Really drove me crazy. I was more of a spontaneous person. Sometimes, I don't like to plan. but for him, everything always had to be planned. So, at times, I would end up doing many things on my own. When Sheyna was single, I would call her and she was always up to it.

"Of course, these things slowed down when my kids were born. By then I had stopped working coz I wanted to be home with the kids. I wasn't really career driven I guess and probably wanted the sort of freedom that not working brought. I did have help though to do the housework and stuff as there was no way I could manage all. Not as superwoman as I thought I might have been", I laughed.

"I really don't know where it all went wrong or if it did go wrong at all. I don't know if time increased my frustration of not being able to do the things that I really wanted to do. I really just got tired of having nothing on my own, having not achieved anything at all in my life and I think it slowly got to me without me realizing it. Funny thing is that I was the only one who couldn't see all that I actually did achieve.

"I know all marriages or relationships evolve as time goes along but evolving to a point where you have nothing to talk about anymore, nothing to laugh about anymore, nothing to discuss anymore was just getting a little too much. There was just not an ounce of excitement anymore.

We tried to talk this through but it always ends up in an argument as my husband does not see it as a problem. He is one of those that believe that since he is doing is husbandly duties of working, bringing food to the table, putting a roof over our heads and providing for the children, then there is no reason to think that anything is wrong in our lives.

As I said, he is not a bad person and he does everything that is required of a husband and a father but emotionally, there was nothing there for me. I will never know though coz in his mind, there is no problem. But in my mind, the problem was brewing. I suppose we are just different in that way.

"I had everything with my kids. Everything a mother could want from her kids, I had. They were the very reason I never took a step towards anything, until that fateful night. They kept me home."

Tears started rolling out of my eyes. I couldn't control it. He held me close to him. Gave me his handkerchief and as I wiped my eyes, I could smell that familiar smell. Something about the smell caught my attention. I suddenly remembered where I had smelt it before.

My heart started beating and I slowly put the hand I was holding the handkerchief down on my lap. But it cannot be. It just can't be. I pushed it aside.

"You okay?" he asked as he leaned his head on mine.

"Yeah," I said.

"What happened that night?" he asked gently. At this point he was holding me and for some strange reason I just felt secure.

"I really don't know. I don't know why I was so angry. I think that it was all these years of bottled up anger that just came out of me."

I closed my eyes and tried to think of what actually happened that night. I'm trying to think of what was the exact cause of my meltdown but nothing specific came to my mind. It was just a random argument that blew out of proportion.

"I wanted to do something for myself. I remember that. I wanted to do something that would make me feel useful. I tried to talk to him about it and when he said we'll see, the argument escalated and I don't know why I just lost it."

Tears were just dropping from my eyes. I started to choke on it. I was struggling to breathe. How bad do I sound walking out on my family for such a small issue.

He held me closer and tightened his arms around me. In an almost whisper he said, "Calm down. Just breathe…just breathe…I know what you're thinking and it's not true. You are not a bad person and have never been. You have sacrificed everything that you ever wanted to do for the happiness of those you love. Don't ever forget that."

"Just before I walked out, I was screaming so much to a point that I felt like I was choking. I was struggling to talk. My kids were crying. My husband was trying to reach out to me. He was trying to hold me. My kids were calling me but I just kept moving back. I felt such a sharp pain on my chest and I was still trying to talk but words were just not coming out of my mouth. The scene in my house. I….I just can't get it out of my head. In my mind… I wanted to run to my husband's arms and let him hug me and I wanted my kids to hug me too but I just kept moving back and back till I was out of the house and I just ran."

I could hear his breath. It was that still. Even the flowing water seemed to have silenced. I suddenly felt so tired. I don't know why I just felt like I had no energy left in me. I just wanted to close my eyes and drift away.

"Hey…"

I looked up at him but I just couldn't move.

"You know what hurt the most. It was when I came back home that night and everyone just ignored me. My kids were sitting in the hall just staring at the TV. I tried to talk to them but whatever I said seemed to have bounce off their ears. My husband was in our bedroom lying down on the bed. When I crawled into bed with him, he didn't even flinch a little. I tried to apologize but he wasn't even interested in listening. He just sighed and I cried. I cried coz I was so frustrated, sad and angry. I was angry with you for stopping me."

He sighed and did something that I did not expect at all. He kissed my forehead and as much as I was in shock, I just closed my eyes and let the tears run down my face. I just felt a strange sense of calm.

"Do you believe that things happen for a reason?" he asked.

What an odd question to ask, I thought but I nodded slowly.

"Sometimes it doesn't always have to be a reason that is reasonable to us. It may not be as direct or straightforward as we might like or want it to be but there is always a reason." I could feel him looking at me as he stroked my arm slowly.

I felt so tired. I felt so drained out. I felt oddly weak. So, I just rested back on his chest and closed my eyes. I felt his hand around me in a tight but gentle hug. I must have drifted off to sleep.

I was woken up by this strange feeling in me. It was like a ball of bright light had gone through me and it just felt very warm. I opened my eyes and realized why I must have felt that way. Dusk was setting in. The whole sky was yellow with deep shades of orange splashed all over it and a warm breeze was playing around with the tree leaves making that rustling sound that I love.

"Oh my God, how long did I sleep for? I am so sorry. Were you in this position the whole time?"

Smiling he said, "Don't worry about it. I threw you off a few times and since you were sleeping like a log, you didn't even realize it."

"Very funny. I hope I didn't snore too loud."

"Not too loud," he said.

"What? Noooooo… I snored…oh gosh… how embarrassing."

"Hahahahaha," he laughed. "Was just kidding. You didn't snore at all. You seemed to have had a very peaceful sleep."

Funnily, I yawned. "That would be quite some time since that happened. A nice sleep. I don't even remember dreaming of anything so it must have really been a good sleep."

"You seemed quite tired so I thought I'd let you get some rest."

"Thanks, and I'm truly sorry that you had to sit in that position for so long. Must have not been very comfortable."

"Don't worry about it. It was a pleasure."

I smiled sheepishly. I really felt like a teenager falling in love. This was just so wrong in so many levels but I just couldn't seem to help it. I just wasn't sure if I should wait for him to say something or if I should say it. But I am so scared that if I do and it goes the other way, I don't…wait…why am I even thinking this?

I took a quick glance to the side and I could have sworn I saw him smile, like he knew what I had just thought of.

"You'll be okay?" he asked me and I knew that it was time for him to go. I really wanted him to stay but I didn't know how. Plus, our deal was from Dawn to Dusk.

I swallowed and smiled while nodding. "Yeah. I'm good."

He gave me a kiss on my cheeks and stood up. My stomach knotted at once. I managed a smiled as he playfully ruffled the top of my head and said, "See you tomorrow…honey."

I closed my eyes and immediately froze for a second…I took in a heavy breath and slowly opened my eyes. My heart was racing and my face felt hot. I could feel my heart beat at my throat as loudly as I could hear it…

Maybe I misheard it…maybe I thought that's what he said. It sounded like it but I must be wrong. I did not mention it to him. I did not tell him that part of the story. I know I did not…oh god…I can't be certain… I know I didn't so he could not have known. Which means, I must have misheard it. He said honey…he could not have said Ahaaaniii…

Day 12

I could smell him. As I opened my eyes, he was standing next to me looking at the sky. I wonder why he stood. He normally sits next to me and the first thing I see of him when I open my eyes is his smile. No smile today. Just a look of deep thought. I wonder what that thought is.

"Hey," I said. "A penny for your thought."

He turns to me and sort of chuckles. And he slowly sits next to me. Much closer than he normally does. I don't move. I like the way it makes me feel. I know I shouldn't but I do.

We sit in silence for a while just staring out to space. Watching the sky brighten forcing the shades of colors to disappear as the sun shows itself in full. It's strange how this place never gets hot even when the sun is at its peak. It always seems to be just pleasant at any moment. Like a place that exists only in a dream.

"Are you feeling okay today? You were a little exhausted yesterday," he asked.

"I'm good today. I really don't know what happened yesterday. I mean…but I could be wrong or just imagining it. I feel like I'm getting more and more tired each day, but yesterday was something else. I think I just need to catch up on sleep. I haven't been sleeping well these past few days. I keep dreaming of people singing and it sounds like it's just outside my room door, or more like the room in which I sleep in now. Quite strange actually. I can't really hear any words but it just sounds like a bunch of people reciting something and I'm too scared to look...hahaha."

He laughed but something was not right with him today. I wanted to ask but I didn't know how to ask. He looked a little disturbed or troubled. And nothing was forming in my head to start a conversation. I'm trying to search for something to say but my mind was just blank. Absolutely nothing.

"I wasn't unhappy you know."

"I'm sorry what?" he took my hand and rested it on his lap and leaned back with one hand around my back.

"I said I wasn't unhappy with him. I just don't want you to think that I ran out coz I had a miserable life or something coz I didn't."

"I'm not thinking anything sweetie. I told you from day one, I'm just here to listen. You tell me whatever it is you want to and whatever it is that is in your heart and I'm not judging anything."

"It's really difficult for me to make you understand what I actually feel. There's so much of conflicting emotions that's running through me and have been running through me for so long and I don't know how to sort it out."

"Girl...maybe it doesn't need sorting or maybe it's not as complicated as you might want to believe. Sometimes it just needs telling and maybe it gets sorted out on its own."

I rested my head on his shoulder. And I told him...

Frustration and fear were the biggest downfall in my life. I had so many dreams. I had so many things that I wanted to do but there always...always was something there just blocking me from taking that step. It was like an invisible wall and I don't know why but everything I wanted to do, I would seek someone's approval to do it and never got the nod that I wanted. There was always a reason why it couldn't be done or why it couldn't be done now.

I gave up everything to look after my kids. I thought that I could do something on my own and that would work out well for me. But it was never the right time or why don't I think of something else or any other reason that meant that I couldn't.

I like to travel. My dream is to travel the world. I want to see places. Not just random places but meaningful places. Places with history but yet it's as always never the right time now. Everything will be done when the time was right. It came to a point where I just got sick of it. Sick of asking because it really felt that I had to beg and justify what I wanted only to be told that it was not the right time. But not the right time for whom? Who gets to decide when your right time is?

I thought of leaving so many times but my kids were what stopped me. Fear of them not being able to cope. Fear of them looking for me. Fear of them not understanding the situation. Fear of them thinking that their father is a bad person. And in all fairness, he is not a bad person. He just doesn't really understand. I don't know if he just doesn't understand or it is me that he just doesn't understand.

I think he just assumed that I would not go. I'm quite sure he has no clue why I even left. The one thing I knew was that despite trying to reach out to me that night, I knew in my heart that he would not follow me out of the door and that really broke my heart.

I felt a grip on my waist and turned to him. He had his eyes closed and looked like he was going to say something to me but he opened them and looked up to the sky and shook his head.

"He really is not a bad person. He loved me. I know that for a fact. And I do love him too. I guess maybe I just wasn't in love with him. I don't know if there is a difference between the two. Most of what I know about it is what I had read in books. In reality, I really don't know. We had a lot of good times together and continued to have till that night. It was this frustration in me that was growing and growing and I think it just took over me. I just don't know when it started to consume me."

Tears were just dropping from my eyes. I couldn't stop it. I wanted to but I just couldn't. I felt so guilty it was choking me.

"I did try to seek help. I did try to tell him that I needed to speak to someone but he just wouldn't have it. He just dismissed it by saying...actually he never said anything. He would just make a face and wave it off or tell me not to be silly. I don't think he took it seriously and that's where maybe the problem was."

I was sobbing uncontrollably. He wrapped his hands around me and kissed my forehead. I heard him let out a little sigh. Again, he looked like he was going to say something to me but he didn't.

"I feel like I have cheated him."

"How do you mean?"

"I feel like I got married to him for the wrong reason and I really don't know if he got married to me for the right one. I got married to him but I was not very sure that deep down I was really happy. At that time, it didn't seem to matter. There were many tell-tale signs but maybe I just ignored them as I didn't know how to back off. I was scared that everyone would be angry with me and…"

I buried my face in my palm, "I've made such a mess."

"You keep blaming yourself for everything. Why?"

"How can I not?"

"Have you ever spoken to him about it?"

"No, of course not."

"Why?"

"You don't talk about these things in my house. It's just not done."

"Why did you stay all this while?"

"I told you…my kids."

"What about before your kids? You were happy then? I mean truly happy."

I rubbed my face. And my tears just rolled out again and I choked. "I probably stayed out of loyalty. Now can you see why I blame myself? The fault is mine. I should have been brave to make a decision. I should have been brave to take a stand. I should have been brave to say something. I should have been brave to want to live the life that I want to live but fear as I have told you is one of my biggest downfalls. In anything and everything in my life."

"And the one time I was brave enough to say something, it was for nothing at all and in a split second, I've just ruined the lives of everyone around me. I don't think my kids will ever forgive me for this and that breaks my heart and hurts the most. I love them with everything that I have and I don't know what to do now."

"I can't do this anymore. Every single day since that night I think of them and the pain it causes me I cannot even begin to describe. I want this pain to end. I want it to go away but I made a promise to you…"

I wipe my eyes and I suddenly feel drained again.

"Do you trust me?" he asked.

"What type of a question is that? I come here every day to meet you. I don't know who you are, I don't know where you come from, I've made a promise to you that for whatever reason is important for me to keep…I don't even know your name… and you ask me if I trust you? Really?"

He smiled, "Well…do you?"

I just felt so defeated. I didn't want to argue and I just didn't have the energy for it. I shook my head and looked into the water flowing beneath me and said, "Yes…stranger…I do trust you."

"I will make it better for you."

I turned to look at him and was just about to ask…

"Don't ask me how but I promise you that I will make it better for you but you have to promise me that you *will* keep your promise to me."

Wondering to myself if he was a mind reader, I nodded my head and said I will.

I woke up in a daze. My head was on his lap and I was all curled up.

"Oh *my god*…did I sleep again?" I asked.

He looked at me, smiled and nodded slowly.

"I am so sorry. I really don't know what in the world is wrong with me."

"Don't worry about it. I let you sleep. I didn't want to disturb you. You looked like you really needed the long sleep."

I looked at the sky and realized that it was almost dusk. The sun was slowly pulling back its rays to make way for the grey sky to come which would eventually make way for the dark sky to take over.

"I've wasted the day. I am truly sorry. I just don't know what it is."

He kissed my cheek and smiled. "Don't worry. No day is ever wasted," he said as he stood up. "I'll see you tomorrow."

I was determined to watch him walk away so I turned and waved to him as he was leaving. And then I heard a sound in the water, like something dropped in so I turned back really quickly to see what it was but as I turned back to look at him, he disappeared. Just like that.

I stood up to leave as I got a little freaked out for two reasons. One, I was wondering how could he have disappeared so fast. I barely took my eyes off for two seconds and the second was that in that two seconds, I thought I saw a pair of eyes looking at me from the water. But I know I must be crazy coz there is no chance in hell that I saw that. It must have been a reflection of something. That's the only explanation there is. For the first time since I have been coming here, I suddenly felt a small wave of fear. This place felt so safe all these days.

I shook it out of my mind. Stop it, I told myself. This is your only sanctuary. You start putting these things in your mind and you have nowhere else to go.

But what was that sound. It definitely felt like something had dropped into the water. Maybe it was a stone or something from the trees. Stop thinking about it.

"What has happened, Master? What has made her feel this uneasiness?"

"You might need to tell her the truth sooner than you might have intended to. We have a small situation that can lead to a worrisome outcome', said the calm voice though with a tinge of worry.

"Master, please tell me what is going on. I am starting to get a little too concern for my liking. I feel her uneasiness which in turn is causing mine."

"I have always asked you to trust me…"

"And I always have with no questions…but…"

"I am asking you to trust me fully with all your mind and no questions. It is the only way for the favorable outcome we are hoping for in this situation. I have never let you down and I do not intend for that to happen now. But I need your trust in full with no doubts," said his Master calmly and with full of reassurance.

"You have it, Master. I always have and always will. Just tell me what I should do."

"Sesahana…search within you. You know the answer. You know what must be done and when it must be done given the shift in situation now."

"Yes, Master…"

Day 13

What if I jump now? What if I just put one leg over and just fall in. Or what if I inched a little by little over the edge and just drop in. That way it wouldn't really be my fault. It would be like I just slipped in and fell. The water looks strangely, a little rough today. It seems to be flowing faster than usual. Not so calm as it normally is at this time of the morning where dawn has not come calling yet.

Why are you not flowing calmly? Why are you flowing with agitation? Maybe it's a sign. Maybe I am meant to jump today. Maybe I am not meant to stay for another few days. Three to be exact. Just another three days but why? Why do I need to stay for another three more days? Why do I have to stay for another three more agonizing days?

If I close my eyes and just feel the wind, hear the trees and smell the day, maybe I just lose my balance while doing all this, then it wouldn't count as breaking my promise and I will be free. It would be an accident.

I close my eyes and I could feel the cool breeze sweep across my body and cool my face while playing with my hair, making it dance like the leaves on the trees. I can hear the leaves rustle and I could smell the crisp cool morning air…so fresh that I felt so light and free…a promise broken as I whispered, "Would you really care?"

"Honey…I do care, so please…don't…"

I opened my eyes and turned around to see him walking toward me with his hand reaching out for me.

"Stop…" I said. "Don't you come any closer."

"Sweetie please…"

"You take another step and it won't be an accident."

I could see the strain on his face. I could see his eyes begging. He seemed distracted for a moment and maybe just maybe I thought I saw a little fear run through his eyes. He shifted his eyes very quickly to the side of me and I heard that plop sound in the water again. I turned as quick and looked back at him. He was about to take another step.

"*Don't*," I said.

"What has happened? Why are you so angry?" he asked.

I wasn't sure as well so I didn't know how to answer him. I just stared at him. I just didn't want him to take a step closer to me. I don't know why I was breathing so heavily. I was breathing as if I was so angry but I have no idea why I was so angry. I just kept staring at him and my mind was saying that there was something so familiar about him. I think I was getting frustrated coz I knew there was something about him, especially his smile but I just couldn't put my finger on it and I wanted to know what it was. It was driving me crazy not knowing. I just didn't know why it was bugging me to this extent now.

He ran his hand through his hair but he never stopped looking at me. I could see the frustration in him too. He placed both of his palm on his face and gave a loud sigh. Then he placed his hands in the back pocket of his jeans and cocked his head slightly to his right and said, "Can we please talk?" in a very slow and soft tone.

Guilt was slowly consuming me. Here I was being a real pain and he had no obligation whatsoever to stand there to try and convince me to do anything but there he was trying. I started to feel bad but I just stood there and stared at him. I didn't know what to say. My head was saying sorry but it didn't seem to come out of my mouth.

"Can I please come to you?" he asked while taking a very slow step.

I wanted to nod my head and say yes but absolutely nothing was coming out of my mouth. What in the world was wrong with me?

But because I did not yell at him, I guess he took it as a sign to take another step as slowly as the first one. As he reached nearer to me, I saw him look into the water very quickly and I turned to look but as I did, I lost my balance and suddenly felt his hand on my arm as he twirled me in a quick motion and hugged me tightly as he said, "I got you...I got you...oh god...I got you."

I didn't realize how close I was to the edge of the wooden bridge and I could have sworn that I felt a little tug at my foot before I lost my balance but I couldn't be too sure. It all happened so fast.

I moved slightly back but not breaking his hug and looked up at him and managed to say, "I'm sorry. I am so sorry. I...I just don't know what..."

"It's okayay..."

He closed his eyes and seemed to have drifted somewhere a little while.

"You have to find a way to tell her," the calm and soothing voice said.

"What or who did I see, Master?"

"In time, I will explain but for now it is of grave importance that you find a way to tell her and make her understand or the consequences will be too great ."

He opened his eyes and looked at me and I could tell that something was running on his mind. He looked worried or disturbed. I just couldn't decide which.

"Do you want to take a walk with me?" he asked very carefully.

"Ummm…sure…but where?"

"C'mon, he took my hand and I followed him. I heard that sound again. Something falling in the water and I turned to look but I saw nothing. Just the water calmly flowing by. He saw me looking and motioned a what question with his head and I shook my head quietly.

We walked almost halfway on the wooden bridge and he turned to what looked like a small path leading into the trees.

Suddenly I felt my heart beat faster and a shiver ran down my spine. Just at that moment I thought to myself, *What are you doing? Where are you following him to? If he does something to you, no one would even know where to look for you.*

I stopped abruptly and he jerked as he was still holding my hand. I think he knew what was on my mind.

He came to me and bent down so he was face to face with me. "I am not going to hurt you. I cannot possibly hurt you. You said you trusted me. Did you really mean it?"

I nodded my head and said, "Yes," very softly.

"You wanted to know who I am and now I am going to tell you and show you exactly who I am but you have to trust me completely."

I was starting to get a little more scared. My heart was beating more and I thought that he might have been able to hear it too. My face felt hot. I couldn't take my eyes off him. He didn't look like an enraged psycho but then again, most of them don't.

"Will you trust me completely?"

I nodded my head again I think more in fear than anything else. You watch all these horror movies and every time a situation like this happens, it seems that the best thing to do would be to agree. I can't believe that I am basing my decisions on movies.

I took a deep breath and slowly let it out with my eyes closed. What have I got to lose anyway. Either way I am going. I was hoping it would be on my terms but I guess any term counts.

He turned to walk and I followed. Not that I had much of a choice since he was still holding on to my hand.

We walked through the trees. Just then the breeze swept by and the leaves started to move and make their sound. Gold lights from the rays of the sun were bouncing off the leaves and I smiled when I saw that, not knowing what to expect after this.

"It's pretty isn't it?"

We stopped and I looked around and saw the most beautiful garden I think I have ever seen in my life. Not man-made but just natural. It was like we were in the middle of a hidden world surrounded by all these huge trees. There were so many different types of flowers around. So many colors.

Some were on the grass itself. Some were on the creepers climbing up the trees. And there was just a beautiful smell. A scent that I have never smelt before. I wasn't sure if it was coming off one flower of if it was a combination of everything. All I know was that it was just beautiful beyond words.

I turned to him…

"It's my escape place…"

"It's like a dream place…just like the place with the wooden bridge," I said.

He smiled. Normally his face really lights up with his smile but I could see a small amount of sadness today.

He let go of my hand slowly and turned away and took a few steps away from me. I didn't know what to expect. I was almost certain that something hard was going to come from behind but I was too scared even to guess so I closed my eyes and tried to imagine the pain and get ready for it.

"I am not going to kill you…"

That's when I opened my eyes and got angry again. I turned around flaring, "How do you do that? How do you keep doing that? How do you know?"

"Because I am not what you think I am…"

"Oh God," I said more to myself. I put both hands on my head and I started to cry. "I can't do this anymore. I just can't do this anymore. I shouldn't have listened to you. I should have never wasted these fourteen days. Now that I thought I might have had a reason to change my mind and it turns out, you are just my hallucination. I have just imagined you. All this for nothing…"

I just fell to the ground crying and sobbing. I was so disappointed with myself. How could I have fallen in love with my hallucination? I felt so stupid.

At that moment, my head started spinning. I looked up and felt everything spinning and I could hear these sounds. Like a song being sung by a group of people. Only thing is it didn't sound like they were singing…it was more like reciting or the chanting of something. I felt a little nauseous. I wanted to stand up but I couldn't. The sounds were getting louder and I closed my ears. I tried to block it out but I couldn't. They kept going on and on…

I was trying to use my hand and support myself so that I could stand up…when I felt his hand on my arm. Tears were just rolling down my cheeks. His touch felt so real and I just wanted it to last.

"I am not your hallucination. I am as real as you are."

I started feeling weak again. I couldn't seem to control my tears. My stomach was knotting…my heart felt so much pain. I wanted to scream but I just didn't have the energy to. I kept crying and crying.

"Shhhh…please stop crying, Sweetie. I promised you that I will make it better for you and I will but I do not have the power to take away the awful sadness that is to come first. Please…I'm begging you with all my heart, to just trust me. I will make this better."

"How…? How can you possibly make this better? And what do you mean by the sadness…" And the reciting/chanting kept getting louder. "Do you hear that? Can you hear that?… It's so loud…please make it stop," I was trying to close my ears but the sound just wouldn't go away.

He hugged me. He was still behind me. I was leaning on his arm with my eyes closed now. I was just so tired and weak. I could hear him take a deep breath and sigh heavily.

"I'm going to take you back to that night."

"What?"

"Just trust me…"

Oh my god…I can see myself. Where am I? I feel like I'm floating but I can see myself talking to my husband. I must be dreaming. How else is this possible?

I suddenly see myself shouting and crying. My husband is trying to calm me down but I'm not listening. I am so angry with him. My kids are standing behind him and calling me. I'm struggling to breathe. I'm gasping for air and I'm in pain. I can see myself clutching my chest. I kneel down in pain and I'm lying down in a fetal position still holding on to my chest. He is coming toward me but I'm moving back toward the door and I just keep moving back in tears and I go out the door.

He doesn't come after me because…no…no…no…it cannot be. How is this possible…I've gone out the door but I'm still lying there on the floor in a fetal position. He is shaking me. He is crying and my kids are screaming and calling out for me to wake up…oh my god…he's trying to revive me but I'm just lying there motionless. He is screaming and hugging me. My kids are screaming and crying and they are all hugging me and calling out to me to wake up…

"*Noooooooooooooooooooo…*" I screamed and opened my eyes. I looked straight into his eyes and broke free and ran away from his arm. I kept running but I was not reaching the trees. It's like the more I ran toward it, the further the trees were backing up.

"Stop running…please stop," I could hear him behind me but I wanted to run away as far as I could. So many things were running through my mind. I don't know what I was feeling anymore. I felt so lost. I wasn't even sure where I was running to.

"*Ahaaniii…stop…*"

And at that moment, I stopped dead at my track and slowly turned to face him.

"*Who are you? Why are you doing this to me?*" I asked in such bitterness that it scared me.

He was almost near me.

"*Stop…*just stop where you are. I'm asking you again…*who are you?* I never told you that part of the story…how did you know?"

"If you calm down and just let the anger pass and look at me, you'll see who I am, you'll know who I am."

My breathing was slowing down but I didn't blink away from him. I saw him walking toward me and as soon as he smiled, I knew who he was. I closed my eyes and thought of the beach and as he held me close to him, I knew exactly why his smile and his smell was so familiar to me.

"What have I done to my family? I have destroyed them. How will they ever forgive me?"

Suddenly everything started to make sense.

They didn't ignore me when I came back. They couldn't see me. They didn't know I was there. They were not watching TV, they were just staring blankly at the TV which was covered in white cloth as were all the mirrors and glass cabinets at home.

My husband did not ignore me when I walked into our room. He didn't know I was there too. He didn't hug me coz there was no one sleeping next to him. He cried himself to sleep and I didn't hear it coz I was too angry.

Sheyna, I shook my head as I thought… she wasn't talking to me. She looked right through me coz she didn't know I was there. She was just ranting out her frustration thinking I was around listening to her. She didn't know that she had chosen the correct day. I was listening to her.

I broke away from his hold.

"How do I make this right? Oh God…what have I done?"

"You haven't done anything. It was time for you to come home," he whispered.

"They will not see it that way. They will always think that I abandoned them."

"Not really. Look. What did you do when someone close passed on? You go through all the emotions but in that world, you know that no one has control over it. Then you forgive them and you move on and learn to live with the loss."

"What do you mean in *that world*? Oh my god…am I a ghost? Oh No…are you a ghost?"

"Well…I wouldn't say ghost though some of them do classify us as that. Sometimes spirits and sometimes by others."

"This is not funny…" I buried my face in the palm of my hand and cried again.

"Ahaaniii…"

"*Why*…do you keep calling me that?"

"In our world, that's what you're known as. That's why I wanted you to remember that always so you'll know it was me when I came for you."

"Wha…what do you mean came for me…this is all so very confusing. Nothing is making any sense."

"If you let me, I can take you back to that night again and maybe this time, you can see it from a different perspective since you already know what to expect."

"I'm so tired and confused and sad and I just want this to stop."

I could still hear the reciting/chants but I was just so beat, I didn't mention it. I closed my ears and just rocked myself back and forth. I just felt like I was losing my mind and I would get up any moment now and be at the wooden bridge. Why didn't I just take that step?

"We don't have to if you don't want to."

The sound stopped. It was quiet again. Dusk had come and gone and he was still here with me. It was all dark again but it was quiet. I looked up at the sky and saw the twinkle of the stars. They were so bright against the dark. A breeze rattled the trees and I could hear the sound it made as it swept through them. I took a deep breath.

"Take me back to that night but after I walk out of my house. I have to deal with this."

"Close your eyes," he whispered as he kissed my cheeks gently.

I saw myself walking through the door and running…fast. I was just about to follow me but something caught my eyes and I stopped. I saw a shadow at the side of my house. It looked like it was glowing. I floated toward it and that's when I saw him standing there. Watching me run and he followed me.

I opened my eyes and looked at him.

"You were there."

He nodded. "I was waiting for you. But things didn't go as how I thought it would. I was supposed to take you with me. You have no idea how long I have been waiting for you but everything turned upside down."

"What do I do now?" I asked softly.

"You have to go home as you've been doing but now you'll know exactly what to do. You'll be able to see things as they are and not what you thought they were."

"I'm scared. I don't know what to expect. I'm just…oh …I'm just not sure if I can handle this on my own."

"You won't be alone. When you need me, just close your eyes and talk to me. I'll be able to hear you and you'll be able to hear me too. I cannot come with you, I'm sorry."

I sighed, "It's okay. I understand. This is something that I have to do on my own. Just be there when I need you."

"Always…"

I was in the garden of my home. Just standing there and watching my house. I watched some of our family members leave my house. Hugging and comforting my husband and kids at the porch as they left. I walked up the steps leading to the porch. No one could see me.

I went to stand next to my kids and husband. Watched the people leave. Both my kids turned around and looked straight at me and for a minute I thought that they could see me. I smiled but then realized that they couldn't. They both looked at each other and then to my husband. He smiled at them and nodded his head and all three smiled and I could see them wiping tears away. My heart broke.

I walked back into my home with them. They started to clear the house and put the furniture back in place. They went into the kitchen and helped my husband clear up the dishes and keep the food back in the fridge. Like clockwork, they cleaned everything up before heading up the stairs to their respective rooms. I saw my husband take a look around the house before he headed up to our room.

Standing there and looking all this, I just didn't know what to feel or how I felt. And staring at a photo of me all covered in flowers and garlands was the strangest feeling I felt. Now I knew what the reciting/chants were. Now I know exactly what was happening. It has all become clear to me.

I slowly walked up the stairs. I went into my eldest bedroom and heard her sobbing. I saw my youngest in her sister's bed as well. They were both hugging each other and crying. Tears crept down my face as well. *How do I make it okay for these two kids?* Just then, they both sat up on the bed and looked around the room. I froze. I could see them sniffing the air. I wasn't sure what was going on. I just stood there and waited for them to fall asleep.

I walked out of the room and went into my bedroom. My husband was sleeping with his hand on my part of the bed as if he was hugging me. He couldn't fall asleep without hugging me. I went closer to the bed and saw one of my nightgowns, the one that is his favorite, clutched in hand. I wanted to scream my head off. I was in so much of pain. My stomach started to knot in pain, I was choking and my tears were just flowing.

I ran out to the balcony in our room and sat on the chair. It overlooked our garden and I stared into blank space. It was a clam night. Everything was still. The sky seemed extra dark but the stars were in millions just twinkling in a rhythm. I just sat there looking at them.

Day 14

Sitting by the bridge again, just staring down at the water and watching it flow wondering what is next. A hint of light broke through the sky and I could see its reflection in the water. Just at that very second, I felt a hand on my shoulder. Now, I am not surprised anymore as to how he suddenly appears and disappears. He take a seat next to me.

"Are you okay?" he bumps his shoulder against mine.

"I really don't know what to make of this."

"You know what has happened to you right?"

"Yes. I just don't know how to deal with it."

"That's what I am here for. I will help you go through it."

I let out a sigh. "What were you doing at my house that night?"

"I told you. I came to take you. I made a promise to you that I will come for your life after life to be with you if I had to but it didn't go as planned."

He must have sensed that I was a little confused.

"Look…when we come here for whatever reason that we come and it is time for us to leave, our Guardian will always come to accompany us back home."

"So, you are my guardian?"

"Well…not quite."

I shook my head. "Trust this to be a little more complicated for me than for the others. My life story."

I could see him thinking very hard how to explain this to me and I was wondering if there was a way.

He turned to me and let out a long breath, "If we were back home, you would know exactly who I am."

"That doesn't really help me much. We are here and I have no clue."

"Fair enough," he said.

"What do I do now?" I asked him.

"You could make things right with your best friend" he cocked his head a little to look at me.

"How do I do that? I mean, I cannot speak to her and given what has happened to me, if she sees me, she'll be sitting here with me as well."

"Hahaha…funny even in the most bizarre circumstances. That's your gift actually. You see the light even in the most difficult situation."

"Hmmm…I think I lost it somewhere along the way."

"It happens but eventually you find it back somehow."

"So, what do I do? How can I make it up to her?"

"Do you know why you love the breeze so much?" he smiled.

"How did you know that?"

"There is nothing about you that I don't know, Ahaaniii."

I want to know but I am scared to ask. I don't know why I am scared after all that I have seen but I can't seem to ask him what I want to ask so again I defer…

"Go on…tell me why I love the breeze so much."

"Coz you feel it. You cannot see it but you feel it so you know that it is there. The breeze is something that doesn't fall into the…seeing is believing…category. You don't need to see it to believe it…you need to feel it and you know it is there…and that is how you can make it up to Sheyna. She doesn't need to see you…she just needs to believe that you are there."

"My kids…last night…for a moment I thought that they saw me…is that how…I mean…did they feel me?"

He nodded his head while smiling. "They could smell you to be more accurate. They got your perfume scent."

"*Oh my god*…in the room…that's why they fell asleep more peaceful. That's why they had smiled at each other…they felt me…I made them feel better," I started tearing up again. "What about my husband? Did he know I was there? He was asleep when I got to the room…did he know? Did he feel me? Can I do that again tonight when I go back?"

"Yes…you can do that whenever you want to. There are other ways too."

"Like how?"

"Come. Let's go pay Sheyna a visit. Close your eyes and just think of her."

I felt his hand on my back and I felt light like a feather. Before I knew it, he was asking me to open my eyes and there we were standing just outside Sheyna's gate that leads to her garden and the porch to her house. I saw her sitting on the rocking chair that's on her porch. White rattan ones that we picked out together to spend our afternoons just drinking and talking. She had her eyes close and one hand was on the empty chair rocking it together as she rocked hers.

I took a step back and felt his body behind me. He held my waist and I leaned back on him and thought to myself…what can I say to her. What could I possibly say to ease her pain?

"You don't have to say anything. Just go there and she'll feel you."

I took a step forward but turned to see him smile and nod his head. I know he didn't say what he said out loud but I heard it in my mind. I wasn't sure if he was nodding for that or acknowledging that I was going to walk over to Sheyna. I'll ask him later.

As I walked, the breeze came softly and rustled the leaves as it always does. The wind chimes on her porch started making their sounds and as I reached the stairs to the porch, she stopped rocking and looked at me. I knew she couldn't see me.

She looked up at the wind chimes that she had and the little one with the hearts that always gave out the best chime was my favorite. It was making the most sound. It was as if the breeze was helping her to tell her that I was there. It seemed to be circling that wind chime the most.

I looked back to see if he was still there. He was. Just standing there and watching me.

I climbed up the stairs and sat in the empty chair. She continued to rock her chair and the one that I sat in too.

"I miss you," she said while crying. "I miss you so bloody much it hurts just to think about it. I don't know how I am going to get through my life without you. We've spent half of our lives together. We were supposed to grow old together. You and me. Oh god…please come back…pleeeaassseeee… I need you… I can't do this on my own."

Seeing her cry just made me choke. I wanted to run out of there. I didn't know what to do. *I just can't do this.* I stood up...

"Ahaaniii...don't...you can do this. She really needs you."

I looked at him. How does he do that? How is he reading my mind?

"What do I do? I don't know what to do..."

"Look at the wind chime."

As I looked at it, a light breeze came about and passed through the heart chime and I saw Sheyna looked at it and smiled.

"She doesn't need to see you to know you are there, Ahaaniii...she just needs to feel you. What would you do if you were there right now in that life?"

I walked behind her chair. She had stopped rocking it to look at the chime. I leaned over and gave her a big tight hug and a kiss on her cheek.

A big gust of wind blew into the trees and swayed them from side to side. The wind chimes were also set in motion swaying while chiming away. But above all the little one with the heart was bouncing off the sun's rays and projecting hearts all over the walls on her porch.

She closed her eyes and took a deep breath and let it out.

"I can feel you. I know you are there. I might not be able to see you but I know I can feel you. I can get your smell too... If you can hear me, I just want you to know that I love you so very much and I will miss you with all my heart for everyday that I live. But I also want you to know that I promise to look after the kids and him for as long as I live. I will always be there for them and I will fulfill all their dreams as how you would have."

I hugged her and I could feel the warmth between us. I wasn't sure if she felt it to.

"I know you will…I love you too for eternity and I'll be waiting for you. You're gonna be fine…you're gonna be okay…"

"I'll be okay now," she said as she looked at the wind chime and the hearts all over the porch wall.

I sat down with her for a little while more as she rocked her chair and mine to the faint sound of the wind chimes, the rustling of the tree leaves and the feel of the breeze.

I stood up to leave. I turned to her not knowing what to say when I heard her…

"Goodbye my friend…till we meet again," she smiled and looked at the sky.

With that I felt like a heavy load had been lifted off my shoulders. I suddenly felt light and one part of me felt really happy.

I walked to her. Kissed her on her cheeks and said goodbye to her. As I walked down the stairs, the little heart chimed once again and I knew she and me would be okay…

I ran to him. He was standing where he left me and I was just so happy to see him that I ran into his arms and gave him the biggest hug. I just felt like some of my pain had been taken away. And just for that moment, I wanted to feel free of that pain even if it was just some of it.

He kissed my forehead and said, "Close your eyes…"

I did and when I heard him tell me to open them again, we were on the wooden bridge.

We sat at the edge of the bridge like we always did.

"What's next?" I asked him.

"Well, it depends on which path you take."

"What do you mean which path?"

"Your original path or the alternative path."

"Oh…you mean…in there," I looked down into the water. He said yes.

"But I am already…well… I'm not really living right now so how can I double die?" I said looking into the water again.

"When you left, you made a decision to take this path. Normally, a decision is not made. You follow the path. But when you made that decision, you deviated from the norm so now it is up to you to choose where you go. I cannot make that decision for you."

"Oh, I see…I have complicated things for myself now."

"It's not complicated. You just have to decide. Down there or you follow me," he said with a little disappointed tone. Maybe because after so much, I should have already made a decision and the fact that I am still contemplating must be making him mad.

"Are you mad that I have not decided?"

"Ahaaniii…it's not my place to be mad. I promised to accept whatever decision you make after the sixteen days and I have to keep that promise. I can only hope," he seemed a little sad.

I felt bad. I know that I have already made my decision, but I feel bad for not telling him yet. "How many days do I have left?"

"Two…"

I nodded. "Has there been a case where anyone chose…you know…down there?" I pointed at the flowing water.

"Yes…just one…"

"Oh…and what happened?"

"I don't know…we don't know…it's not spoken of."

"I see…"

I took a deep breath and slowly let it out. "These two days that I have, is it just to make a decision or do I have only two days to be here?"

"To make a decision. If you choose neither, then this will be it. How you are right now until you make a decision as to which path you will follow."

"So…I'll be here aimlessly…"

"Yes…they will move on Ahaaniii…they will carry on with their lives. That's just the way things are. You will always be part of their lives but you will not be in their lives physically."

"Will I be able to make it better for them like I did for Sheyna before I go?"

"Definitely."

"Can I make it better for my siblings, my nephews and nieces as well?"

"For sure. You can make it better for anyone you want to, Ahaaniii…"

"Will you take me like you took me to Sheyna's?"

"Sweetie, I'll take you anywhere you want to go in these next two days to make it better for anyone and specially to make it better for you."

Dusk was settling in. The shades of colors were slowly disappearing giving room for a grey sky to take over. The breeze swept smoothly across and the leaves on the trees danced away…I felt it move across my face and felt a little chill over my body.

A tear escaped my eye and rolled down to my cheek. And a few more after that. I slowly wiped it off with the back of my hand. He slid his hand across my waist and pulled me close to him and as I laid my head on his shoulder, I could hear the reciting/chanting but this time it sounded so bliss. I stared out into the disappearing greying sky that was making way for the darker sky with the twinkling stars. The night was beautiful.

"I have to go," I told him.

He smiled and stood up with me. "I'll see you tomorrow," he said as he gave me a kiss on the forehead. I watched him walk all the way and fade into the distance. Not surprised anymore.

I looked back at the water and the trees in the distance and closed my eyes to the smell of nature and the feel of the breeze and thought of my home. I took a deep breath and let it out slowly. I opened my eyes to my husband and kids cleaning the house as they did yesterday.

As I turned to look at them, I saw the three of them smile at each other, as if to acknowledge my presence. They could get my perfume smell. I walked around the house knowing that I will only be here less than two days. I would miss them all but they will move on without me. Will I watch over them from where I am? I really hope that's how it works.

Day 15

Day fifteen, I thought to myself. The cold breeze sent a little shiver across my body. It felt like a big day today but I don't know why it felt that way. Was something big supposed to happen today? I closed my eyes to take in the surrounding. Sound, smell, feelings…everything around me. I caught a whiff of a familiar smell and smiled.

I felt a kiss on my cheek. I opened my eyes to him smiling at me. I've grown to love that smile over the past fifteen days. It was comforting, reassuring and it felt like there was so much love in that one smile.

"Hi…" I said.

"Hey…are you okay?"

"Hmmm…coming to terms with the loss of myself…"

"Hahaha…somehow you always seem to find humor in the strangest situations," he said.

I looked into the flowing water. "I think it was my defense mechanism in life. I hated being sad and I hated sad situations. Never really knew how to deal with them so I make some joke out of them thinking that it will be less sad. Deep down I don't think it really worked. Maybe just on the surface."

I saw him looking down into the flowing water but it was as if he was searching for something. I continued to just look at him but he didn't realize that I had stopped talking. A good minute passed before he turned to me and I found myself arching one eyebrow with a quizzical face.

"I'm sorry," he said.

"Were you looking for something in there?"

"Umm. *No*…Ahhhh…I'm sorry. I heard what you said but for some reason, I got distracted."

"By the water?" I asked arching my eyebrow again.

He rubbed his forehead and shook his head. "I'm truly sorry. I didn't mean to seem like I was not paying attention. I really did hear you."

"Hey…no worries. I'm not offended or anything. Just curious as to what might have caught your attention in the flowing water."

"It's nothing really. I'm sorry again."

"I feel like something is going to happen today," I said.

"How'd you mean?"

"I mean…I feel like today is a big day. I don't know for what but it just feels like it. You know…it's like…hmmm… how can I explain this," I said thinking.

"Do you feel some uneasiness or something?"

"No…quite the contrary…you know…it's like you've been in a messed-up situation for some time and suddenly you wake up one day and just feel like today everything will work itself out."

I look at him. "Do you understand what I'm trying to say?"

"Does it feel like a closure to something?"

"Yeah…yeah…that's it…that's what it feels like. It feels like there's a closure to something but I'm not sure what."

"I turn to look at him and immediately realize and say, 'But you know what…"

He looks at me.

"You know exactly what," I say to him.

He nods his head and slowly says, "Yeah…I know what."

"Ahaaniii…you have till tomorrow…to decide which path you take. I cannot interfere in that decision that you make," he sighs sounding a little sad.

For a split second I had almost forgotten what he was talking about. Then it hit me…the circumstances in which we met. *He still thinks…but how? I mean…I'm already gone…what good would it do to jump now?* My situation kinda defeats the purpose.

"Oh…" I said. "Ummm…not trying to sound stupid or anything but I'm sorta new to this situation of…well…not being alive, but I thought you would have already figured out which path I'm gonna take given that I don't really have a choice of any other path."

He chuckled and looked at me. Shaking his head and laughing a little, "Oh God…you find the oddest time to crack someone up."

"Do I have a choice?" I ask him now a little more on a serious note.

He looks up to the sky and lets out a slow heavy breath… "Yes…yes you still do."

"But how? How do I have this choice?"

"Ever heard of the term Lost Souls?"

"Yeah but definitely in a different context. I mean…that just means that you haven't found what you want to do in life or you're just wondering about aimlessly or something like that. Not dying and becoming lost."

He chuckled again…

"What would happen if I did go down there?" I pointed to the water with my head.

I could see his body and jaw tighten a little. He took my hand and placed hit on his lap, "Honestly, I don't know. We have only ever lost one and we don't know what has happened."

"We? Who is we?"

"Ahaaniii, tomorrow at dusk will be your final journey. All the questions you have in your mind will be answered depending on which path that you take. I can only lead you through one," he said looking straight ahead. I heard him sigh and turn to me…

A shiver ran through my spine. This tingly feeling was running through my body and my stomach was knotting. My face felt hot and I think I was blushing. I don't know how all these were happening but it was.

I turned to look at him and before I could say anything, I felt his hand on my waist and his lips on mine. My mind was in turmoil as I parted my lips to the warmest and longest kiss I've felt since I cannot remember when…it was made perfect with the breeze slowly sending a nice amount of cold, the trees dancing the right amount of sway, the leaves rustling the right amount of sound and the sun giving out the right amount of golden rays. It felt so magical…like a dream but real at the same time.

I didn't want it to stop. I just wanted it to carry on for eternity.

He rested his forehead on mine and as his heavy breathing was slowing down, he traced the side of my face with his finger and rested it on my neck. He slowly cupped my face in both of his hand and said, "I love you with everything that I have and no matter what it takes, I will find you, life after life."

At those words, my heart started pounding so hard. I moved back from him and stared into his eyes. I could see the beach, I could see the smile, I could get the scent and I could hear the words…

"*Oh my god*…it was you…it was you that day at the beach years ago…"

I didn't know how to feel. I was not sure if I was angry or happy, if I wanted to laugh or to cry.

"The one and only," he said with both his hand out as if in a courtesy.

I think I was stunned into silence coz I wanted to say so many things and ask so many questions but nothing was coming out of my mouth so I just sat there in silence.

"Please say something sweetie," he said as he held my hand.

"Explain."

"Ok…each of us have a guardian when we are out of our world, if you would like to call it that. I am yours. Except that I am not just your guardian but I am also your soulmate."

I look at him with blank in my mind. I couldn't even think of anything.

"Ahaaniii…you might not see it now, but there is a reason why you never let me out of your mind all those years and why you remembered your name when I told it to you. That connection between us is there but you have to let go of what you have here in order for you to see it…to feel it."

"Where did you go all these years? Why did you not come looking for me?"

"I have always been around you. I did not come back in this form. I only did it once, that day at the beach. I was only allowed to do that once and now. I needed you to remember me. To come back with me."

"What is your form then?" still blurred out and blanked.

"It's not just my form, it's our form. Should you decide to follow me tomorrow, we'll go together in the same form."

"Why do you still think that I am yet to make a choice?" I turn to him and rested my head on his shoulder. I could feel his shoulders rest in ease and heard a small sigh of relief.

You have done well Sesahana. Bring her home tomorrow.

We sat in silence for a little while and I knew that I had some unfinished business to take care of before I leave for what might seem for good.

"Do you want me to come with you?"

I shook my head and bit my lips. "I think I have to do these next two days on my own."

He nodded. "Just call me if you need me. I'll be there."

"You know…I look back at my life and it just feels like I have achieved nothing. I was so busy chasing something and thinking my life would start once I got it, that I completely forgot to live."

"Don't say that."

"But it's true. There were so many things that I wanted to do but I just kept putting it off for some reason or the other or was made to put it off for some reason or the other that I never got around to do what I dreamt of doing."

"True as that may be…you did raise two kids who turned out great, kept your marriage going thru all the turmoil that was going through your mind and created a happy home for your family. I know it doesn't seem much in your eyes, but believe me some people don't even have that to go on."

I knew what he was saying was true. Many a times I thought that to myself but it had never been any comfort to me knowing that. I really wished I had pushed for something that I wanted. Anyway, it's a little too late now.

The calm flowing water seemed a little agitated again. I tilted my head and looked at it with a questionable look and looked at him. He tried to mask it but I saw the change in his expression. I decided to pursue it instead of keeping quiet.

"The water flow has changed. This is the second time it has happened. It's not as calm now. Did you notice it?"

"Yes. I did."

"Hmmm…strange," I said. "Anyway, I have to go. I have some things that I need to make okay before I leave tomorrow," I said as I stood up.

He stood up with me. We looked up at the sky and watched dusk creep in along with my friend the breeze. Always making itself present just at the right time.

He turned to face me and he pulled me close. He kissed my forehead and rested his head on mine. He then placed his finger under my chin and slowly lifted my head to face him and the warmth of the kiss just transported me to everywhere and nowhere. Once again, I did not want it to stop but I knew that it would.

He slowly broke the kiss and looked at me. There was just so much of love in his eyes and it gave me a strange feeling in my heart. I suddenly felt that I couldn't wait for tomorrow. I felt light. Like all my problems had just melted away. And mostly, it just felt that my family will be okay without me. I don't know how all that feeling came just from his eyes. I cannot explain it. But it did.

As he walked away, I closed my eyes and found myself back at home watching my husband and kids clearing up. My siblings were also there. They were sitting on the floor and looking at my photo that was set on the table decorated with flower garlands and baskets of flowers all around. It was very pretty.

But I could see them tearing slowly. I knew what I had to do. I walked over and sat right in front of them. I knew they couldn't see me. I closed my eyes and tried to speak to their mind. I told them that everything will be okay and that they should not feel sad. They should be happy for me. I know they will miss me and I will miss them too but life has to go on.

Then I slowly stood up and went and hugged them one by one. A moment of recognition hit them. Recognition of my perfume smell perhaps as they looked at each other and smiled.

I saw my kids sitting at the dining table, watched them smile and heard my elder one say, "You got the smell didn't you. You got Mummy's perfume smell. She's here. I know it." My youngest was smiling and nodding her head in agreement.

All of them nodded in silence and smiled.

I didn't know what to do then. Should I stay? Should I go?

Then I heard the doorbell. At first I thought it was strange that anyone would come at this time of the night. Then I looked around the room and understood what was about to happen. It was my final send off. This was our custom. I knew exactly who was at the doorstep. He would be the one who everyone thinks will help me cross over to the 'other side' as the living would say.

I stayed for the sake of my husband, kids, siblings, family members and friends. I watched them do the preparations. I heard them talk about me. All the things they would miss about me. All the things that they would miss me doing for them. Just at that moment, I wished I could have participated in the conversation. I wished I could tell them that I would miss them too with all my heart and that everything would be okay.

Some of my relatives though…I wish I could haunt them. Just thinking about it made me laugh. It would be cruel to suddenly just show up and make myself be seen though I wasn't sure if that was possible, but it would be really funny coz they would have definitely deserved it. I felt terrible laughing in my head. Well, technically, I could have laughed out loud. No one would hear me.

I suddenly felt very light. My feet were on the floor but it felt like I was floating. I looked at it again just to make sure I wasn't flying off or something. It was a strange feeling.

I sat in the far corner of the room watching everyone take up their positions in the room facing my beautiful shrine. That's what it looked to me anyway. It was so nicely done. I could see the touches of my elder one.

Then 'The One' started to do what I believe was probably the prayers and rituals to help me cross over and I found the ringing of the bells so comforting. I closed my eyes and listened to them. All sounds drowned out and I could just hear the bells and the chanting. This was the sound that I found so disturbing a few days ago but somehow, they seem so peaceful and serene now.

A few moments later everyone started to chant various hymns. I found myself enjoying this. I wasn't one who was that religious growing up but funny how I seem to like it. This went on for some moment with 'The One' and when he was finished everyone else continued singing religious hymns. Having been to a few of these during my lifetime, I knew exactly what was going to happen next.

When the last hymn was sung, there was a moment of silent. Then everyone got up to go and have the food that was contributed by so many people.

I still sat in the corner watching. My husband...my kids...they were occupied now but the hardest moment I knew would come after tomorrow. I have to let them know that it will be okay. They will get through this and move on.

I closed my eyes and wondered where he was. I wasn't sure that I was going to be able to move on.

"Don't think that," I heard him say.

I opened my eyes and looked around but did not see him anywhere.

"I'm not there."

"Then, where are you?" I whispered looking around to make sure no one can hear me.

"Why are you whispering?"

"I don't know..."

I heard him laugh.

"It's not funny...how are you doing this?"

Again, he laughed.

"Stop laughing...are you watching me from somewhere?"

"Yes."

"How are you talking to me?"

"Through your mind."

"Why can't I see you then?"

"You'll soon find out."

"What is that supposed to mean?"

"Means it's a little difficult to explain right now but you will know soon enough and you can stop whispering. No one is going to hear you even if you scream."

"What do I do now? How can I make this okay for them?" I started panicking as I realized that I only had less than a day before I'm not even sure what happens but it feels like I will not be here anymore.

"Sweetie…stop panicking. You've got this. Just calm down. All you need to do is wrap your arms around them and say what you want to say to them. They might not be able to hear you but they will definitely feel you."

I saw my little one walk up the stairs to her room and I knew that it was time. I slowly got up and followed her. Again, I started feeling this lightness in me. I kept looking at my feet to make sure that I was still grounded and not hovering. It was grounded. What is this strange feeling?

It felt like I had opened the door when I walked in but I turned around and her room door was still shut. *Hmmm…*

I saw her standing by her study table which is placed against the wall where the window is. She was just staring out of it. As I approached her, I saw a framed photo of the both of us in her hand. It was a random shot of me lifting her up over my head. She was a little over three years old then. Her black curls fell to the side of both her cheeks and you could hear her laugh just by looking at her expression in that photo. And I was beaming with pride looking at her.

I saw her tearing and she slowly broke into a quiet sob.

"Oh God...I miss you, Mummy...I miss you so much," she whispered as she cried and held her stomach. Tears were just streaming down her cheeks. I knew that pain. I've cried that cry so many times to know how much it hurts.

My eyes felt like a ton of tears were just going to burst out but I found myself strangely calm as I stood behind her. I put my arms around her waist from behind and I rested my head on her shoulder. She moved her hands away from her stomach and for a split second looked like she was in shock but then she let out a breath and put her hand on my arms and closed her eyes.

"Oh baby...my darling sweet baby. I am so sorry to put you through this."

"I know you didn't mean to mom...I know you didn't mean to."

As I was about to pull back I heard him say, "She can't hear you but she can feel you."

I wished she could hear me. For what felt like the longest time, I just hugged her.

"It's going to be okay. Everything is going to be okay. I will always watch over you and guide you through. You are the bravest little girl I know. And I love you with all my heart and that will never change."

"I love you with all my heart mom. I hope you can hear me coz I really feel like you're with me now."

All of a sudden, I felt warm. I cannot explain it. I suddenly felt warm and full of energy. It felt like I was glowing but I definitely wasn't.

I saw her take a deep breath and look at the photo she was holding. She smiled and kissed the photo and said, "I know everything is going to be okay now."

I slowly slid my hands away from her and watched her walk to her bed and lie down on her pillow. She closed her eyes and I bent over to kiss her one last kiss and watched her smile and go to sleep.

Again, I thought that I had opened the door to my elder one's room but when I looked back to close it, it was not opened at all. Was I walking through doors?

She was already in bed. Her eyes were closed but I knew she was not sleeping. I wondered if she knew I was there. I climbed onto the bed and hugged her.

I was about to tell her that everything was going to be okay when I heard her sniff and sigh. I saw her wipe her eyes with a tissue that was in her hand…

"I don't know if you can hear me mom but I'm pretty sure you're around somewhere. I am not sure if I am imagining or not but I really do feel you."

I closed my eyes and wished to god that I could tell her that I was there but I couldn't. I felt that glow again. That warmth and glow. It was such a ticklish feeling.

She stirred and turned around to face me. It really felt like she was looking straight at me but I knew she couldn't see me. Nevertheless, I didn't move a muscle except to continue hugging her.

As she closed her teary eyes she whispered, "I know you didn't mean to go mom. I know you didn't want to go. Someone must really love you to bits from up above to take you but I just want you to know that everything is going to be okay. We will all be okay. You have thought us to survive and we will. I just want you to know that all your teachings and advice will not go to waste. I will make sure of that."

I was choking not with tears but with pride. My elder one has stepped up in just a matter of days. One last hug, one last kiss was all I wished I could give. I looked at her and saw her tears streaming down her face.

As she took the tissue to wipe her tears she said, "Wherever you need to go to mom, please go with a peace of mind. Don't feel sad or guilty and don't hold on. We know you will guide us and we know you will always love us and shine on us."

I gave her a kiss on her forehead and hugged her for the longest time and when I thought she fell asleep, I crawled out of the bed, looked at her and knew that it will be alright.

I walked out of the room and realized that I had walked through the door so when I went into my bedroom, I didn't look back at the door as I already knew how I had got in.

I saw him on the bed. Lying on his back and looking blankly at the ceiling. As I got nearer to the bed, I saw the tears falling to the sides of his face. He was breathing heavily to control himself from crying but the tears were flowing.

I sat on the bed at the side of him. I didn't know what to say to him. I moved in to lie next to him and put my head on his chest. Again, I felt that glowing warmness. I closed my eyes and only then did I feel how much I was going to miss him. My stomach knotted. I wished he could feel me, my touch.

"If you are here, like I feel you are," he said.

I opened my eyes and said, "Yes, I am but you can't see me, you can't hear me and I want you to see me and hear me. I am going to miss you." I started crying and I just couldn't control myself. *What have I done? How did it come to this? I don't even get a second chance here.*

"I know you didn't want to go," he continued. "I know it was not your time. You still had too much of life in you but I guess whoever is up there felt otherwise or knows better."

I sat up and looked at him.

"If you are listening to me, I just want you to know that all will be okay. You have brought the kids up well. You have taught them well. If you need to let go to find your peace, then go ahead and let go. We know you will watch and guide us from above so don't hold on baby. Go and find your peace. If anyone deserves it, it is you. I will love you with everything that I have till I find my peace."

I leaned forward and gave him the longest kiss though I knew that he could not feel it.

I walked out of the room and just went around the house aimlessly. I saw my siblings sleeping in the guest bedroom and some relatives scattered here and there in the hall. I sat on the floor and looked at my shrine. My mind was blank and I just wanted it to be that way for a while.

Day 16

Dawn today is different. I will not be sitting at the bridge overlooking the water and feeling the breeze while waiting for him to appear out of thin air. Instead I will be watching my family bid a final farewell to me. What an unusual thing to see. But I guess it is unusual if you are amongst the living and maybe not so unusual when you are amongst the non.

Everyone took their places sitting on the floor in front of my shrine. Waiting while 'The One' prepared all the things he needed to make the transition easy for me. I waited too.

Then he started with the bells and the lights and continued with the chanting. He burnt incense sticks and for some strange reason I could smell all these. I was fascinated with the fact that I could smell the fragrance. It was very calming.

Once he finished, someone started to sing a religious hymn and everyone else followed suit. Once that person finished, someone else started another one and everyone else followed suit again. I watched in amazement as my kids attempted to lead a hymn each. I wished they could see how proud I was. My husband tried too. I walked over and kissed them all once.

Once everything was over, I saw 'The One' packing some of the items up in a small cloth and hand over what looked like an urn to my husband. For a split second, I wondered before it hit me that I was in the urn in the form of ashes. For the life of me, I have no idea why I felt sad but I did. I guess I just thought to myself that all my life has suddenly boiled or burnt rather, down to be ashes and a photo.

I watched all the men, headed by my husband, walk toward the front door and finally out of it. They got into the car and I saw them drive away.

All around the house, everyone was cleaning up the house. In the far corner, sitting on a chair, I saw my best friend Sheyna just looking at my photo. I went to sit next to her. I held her hand though I knew she couldn't feel anything. She put her head down and started to cry. "I miss you…I know you didn't mean to leave me…but I'm still so angry because I miss you so much."

I closed my eyes and concentrated on what I am not sure, but I felt that strange glowing warmth again.

"Do you feel her?" my younger one asked Sheyna as I saw Sheyna smile and nod.

"I felt a warmth go through me just for a split second. Wasn't sure if I was imagining it."

"You're not. I felt it too, last night."

"So did I," my bigger one said.

I felt happy. I think I felt happy because I found a way to communicate with them and most of all I think I was happy that they didn't blame me for what had happened. They all still loved me the same.

I looked outside the window and saw the first light crack the dark sky.

I knew there was nothing more for me to do here. They would all find their way and they will be alright.

I walked towards the door. That strange glow and warm feeling was growing stronger. I could feel it. I kept looking at my arms to see if there was any glow on it but there wasn't. I don't know what I was expecting to see. A layer of light over me or something, maybe but I didn't see anything. I could feel it but not see it.

I opened the door, well, I think I did open the door but judging from the no reaction from anyone, I guess the door must have been opened. I walked out to see the sun throwing its golden rays all over the sky and I thought that maybe that was what I was feeling but it wasn't. This glow and warmth was coming from within me.

I looked up at the sky and for a moment, I thought I saw little orbs of faint gold light moving up towards the sky. I blinked to get my eyes in order and looked at the sky again. They were gone. I must have been hallucinating or the sun must have gotten to my eyes.

I looked back at the house and saw everyone busy doing something or the other. I closed my eyes and just at that very moment, my friend the breeze was waltzing by. I could hear the leaves ruffling in the trees and I could feel the rays of the sun dancing through them. I took a deep breath and opened my eyes to this beauty of the breeze that can only be felt but not seen.

It circled me and I caught it breezing into the house. I saw the curtains move to its rhythm and saw everyone in the house take deep breaths and look out of the door with smiles on their faces. They knew I was there one last time. And I smiled and turned around with tears streaming down my eyes and walked. My stomach in knots. A wave of sadness passed through me. *I will miss this life.*

As I walked toward the bridge, I looked up at the sky again and this time, I saw stronger golden colored orbs coming down. Though they were at some distance, it looked much clearer now than it did when they were going up toward the sky. I closed my eyes and shook my head but they were still there when I opened them. *What is going on with me?*

I stood still and closed my eyes again and thought of the bridge. Would he be waiting there for me? I felt a cold wind blow over me and found myself on the bridge a few steps behind from where he was sitting. The same spot where I have sat and waited for him for the past fifteen days.

How did I do that? How did I get from the front of my house to here? I just closed my eyes and…wait…technically I'm no longer living so I guess I could do that. I could just go from one place to another without walking. Well, at least there's one benefit.

I slowly walked towards him. And as I did, I figured out how he used to come without making a single sound. Creepy but exciting at the same time. I smiled.

"Nice to feel your smile," he said.

"You got eyes at the back of your head, Mister?"

"I said feel. Not see."

"Doesn't make it any less creepier," I laughed.

He gave a small laugh.

As I was about to sit next to him, I looked ahead and saw an orb of rainbow color go up toward the sky. *What is going on with me today? Why am I seeing things?* I blinked and looked again and I swear I saw another one. *Damn…this is really such a strange day.* I was beginning to wonder if it had anything to do with 'The One' and all his rituals.

"They are us…coming here and going back," he said as he looked at me and smiled.

That very smile that had accompanied me for the past fifteen days. And suddenly I was afraid of what was going to happen next. *Where will I be going? Will I ever see him again?*

But first, "What do you mean, they are us? Who are you talking about? Are there people around here that only you can see and not me?" I asked beginning to sound a little worried now.

He laughed so much while I just stared at him.

"I'm sorry…I am really sorry…you just have this funny way about you."

I cocked my head and lifted up one eyebrow and smiled.

"Glad you find me very amusing. Now please tell me who were you referring to when you said they are us?"

"The orbs that you see. The bright golden ones coming down are coming here to begin their mortal or human life as they call it, as you did, the lighter golden ones that you see going up are leaving but will return in due time when they see fit and the rainbow ones are leaving for good as they do not have any purpose of returning here."

I think he sensed that I was staring at him with an utter disbelieve. He slowly turned toward me and lifted his head to look at me.

"I am going to come back to those light spheres in a minute but first I would really like to know how are you doing that?"

"Doing what?" he asked truly looking puzzled.

"Really? Do you remember me asking you about the lights?"

"Ohhhhhh…hahahahaha…ok…ok… I know what you mean now."

"And…"

"It's how we communicate."

"Explain further…coz it seems to be one sided."

"Not really…you just don't know that you can do it yet."

"I can?"

"Yup…come here," he said as he moved closed to me. He slowly rested my head on his shoulder. A shiver ran through me. I missed his touch. I could smell that familiar smell.

"Close your eyes and think of me and I am going to say something."

"Okay," I said.

So, I closed my eyes and thought of him. And I heard him. I smiled.

I slowly lifted my head from his shoulders and looked at him. He smiled and I gave him a small kiss on his cheeks. I blushed so much as I felt the butterflies in my stomach. It felt like a first date kiss. I think I caught him blush too.

"So, tell me about the orbs," I asked still leaning against his shoulders.

"That's how we are. That's how we come to this world. The difference in color that you see is because while we are here we use up most of the energy we bring hence the lighter color once we are done. The rainbow color as I said is once you choose not to return to this world anymore."

"What will I be? Which color?"

"That is entirely up to you. The choice to return or not is only yours to make."

"What choice did you make?" I asked.

I chose not to return anymore.

I took a deep breath and sighed it out. *What choice do I make?*

"What is troubling you?" he asked.

"I just feel like I have wasted my life here you know."

"How so?"

"I just don't feel like I have achieved anything in this life. It's always been me wanting to do this and wanting to do that for myself but in the end, it doesn't seem that I did anything at all. But at the same time, it's not like I had nothing in this life. To everyone it would seem that I had it all. It's like I have led a life of everything and nothing at the same time."

I bowed my head and looked at the flowing water and saw the little disturbance I saw a few days back. Just for a split second and when I tried to look for it again, the water seemed to be flowing smoothly.

"Ahaaniii…sometimes…"

"Don't say anything." I suddenly felt that I knew what I needed to do. It was a strong feeling in me. I don't know what came over me. Suddenly the glow felt stronger.

I looked at the sky and saw the sun making way for dusk to come in. A shiver ran down my spine. A shiver of excitement. My last dusk here. The breeze did it's magic again. I closed my eyes and felt it.

I turned to look at him. He looked back at me. Just at the moment I wanted to kiss him so badly. Everything suddenly just felt right.

I stood up. I felt light. I felt like I was floating. Again, I looked at my feet but it was grounded. I wasn't floating.

He stood up after me.

I walked to the railing of the bridge and faced him. "Did you mean it?"

"Every word," he said as he walked toward me. He ran his hand down my arm and the butterflies in my stomach were going wild. My breathing started to get heavy.

He rested his forehead on mine and moved his head toward my ear. "I have loved you for all the lives that I have lived and always will. *You*…are my soulmate." And in that moment, I knew that he was mine too.

"It's time," he whispered in my ear.

"I know," I said softly. I looked around and wondered if I would miss it all.

He slowly slipped his hand around my waist and pulled me toward him. I looked up at him and closed my eyes to the softest kiss. I didn't want to let him go as much as I didn't want him to let me go.

"I will never let you go," he said as he slowly broke the kiss.

"It's time. Are you ready?" he asked softly.

I nodded my head slowly not knowing what to expect.

"Close your eyes," he told me as he rested my head on his chest and I felt a special kind of warm through the cold breeze.

I was light again and I was floating. I opened my eyes and looked down and saw the water below me. I was no longer on the bridge but was hovering above it. I looked at him and saw him smile. He was still holding me.

I didn't know what was happening but it felt nice and right. I leaned back on his chest and I could see the rainbow colors around him and around me as I chose not to return anymore.

I looked down once more to the place and everything in and around it that I have come to love for the past sixteen days. I looked at the flowing water and something caught my eye. I thought I saw a face looking up at me. I blinked and looked again but it was gone.

He must have sensed something as he asked me, "What's wrong?"

"Nothing," I said and smiled.

I felt him pull me closer and all I could feel after that was a strong pull upward toward a magnificent bright light while everything around me became rainbow colored.